Aeon Infinitum
RUN FOR YOUR LIFE

E. Rachael Hardcastle

Copyright © 2018 E. Rachael Hardcastle
All rights reserved.

ISBN: 978-1-9999688-2-3

First Printed in 2016

Curious Cat Books, UK
www.erachaelhardcastle.com

No part of this book may be reproduced except in the event that a passage is used as a quotation, or with the author's permission.

For 'Big Pete':

"And I began: *'you are my ancestor,*
You give to me all hardihood to speak,
You lift me so that I am more than I'."

- Dante

Also by E. Rachael Hardcastle

Finding Pandora

World
Heaven
Infinity
Eternity
The Complete Collection

Aeon Infinitum

Run For Your Life

Other Titles

Forgotten Faith
Noah Finn & the Art of Suicide

Why Are We Here?

'It is hereby decreed, that Agaue Czar and his descendants shall rule, *Aeon Infinitum**, the ark Titan in the face of societal destruction, natural disaster and/or an apocalyptic event.'

– The President of the United States, 2022 AD.

*Performing functions in the operation of the universe, for an infinite stretch of time.

1

Eden Maas

My name is Twelve. It's the prison number they assigned me based on my mental and physical strength, considering my monstrous crimes and probability of escape.

If the overall threat increases as will my number, but so far during my sentence of five months, four days and two hours (*I'm not counting*), Warden hasn't promoted me. The higher you rise, the closer to death you become so I'm pleased I'm only at Twelve. It's hell here, but I'd much rather be in prison than out there for sure.

Outside is *Ad Infinitum*, an inhospitable post-apocalyptic world. Since what the survivors call *Ad Initium Děth* (*but what I call the end of the world*), the remains of the human race has been stuck in Titan, a purpose-built underground ark and my home for the past nineteen years.

I sit cross-legged in my solitary confinement cell. I'm waiting for a voice to confirm I didn't die in my sleep. Not that it wouldn't be a blessing; another day brings endless chores, tiny portions of undercooked food and a severe lack of privacy. At least, for now, I can avoid witnessing the other inmates' suffering.

Like them, even though the darkness is consuming and eternal, I'm thankful the blue and purple patches decorating my body are hidden. Breath freezes as I exhale and the onset of foot rot itches between my toes, but I'm pleased to have escaped the alternative.

Rhythmic footsteps enter our cell block. Each step is musical and planned; taunting, jeering and dispassionate. As the guard enters my cell, the slide of the rusted metal bolt and the jangle of keys send echoes throughout Sector C, prompting other inmates to yell abuse and clang their cups for attention.

"Twelve, Warden's call," says a hoarse female voice before her rough hands drag me to a stance.

Although my fingers are shaking and my legs unsteady, I wriggle in her grasp, squinting as I'm shoved toward the corridor's light.

"That's *not* my name."

The guard draws her baton and strikes my stomach, winding me. The force knocks me against the far wall.

"It is now because Eden Maas was a murderer," the guard says. "She died having refused loyalty to Titan."

Between gasps of air I reply, "I didn't refuse loyalty to Titan, only to Czar."

The guard laughs. I feel her chest rumble and her arms shake as she pins me upright; the only sound to unnerve me since my imprisonment. Then without warning, I'm slammed harder against the wall by her uniformed forearm, thoroughly frisked and led into the candlelit corridor before my eyes fully adjust.

"Whatever you call it, Twelve, treason is punishable by death. Consider yourself lucky. At least you have a chance at survival now, even if it *is* running from mutants".

Violent palpitations drum within my rib cage. I hear the unsteady beating of an adrenaline-fuelled pulse in my head and my sight begins to waver.

"I'm being *banished*?"

The guard reaches for her baton as she replies, "That's right, Twelve. Either go quietly or be taken unconsciously. The choice is yours."

I lean on the cell door and focus on just breathing; inhaling through my nose and exhaling through my mouth until the beating steadies and my sight recovers.

"I don't understand. My sentence was suspended pending further investigation. The Warden said-"

"Warden gave the orders, Twelve, now are we going to have a problem?"

Unsure of my intentions, she draws her iron baton from a holster on her belt. It's an older model that's covered in crusted blood and rust. I hadn't noticed its history before and disgusted, I outstretch a hand, pry my fingers free from the rail and shake my head. There *has* to be another explanation for this.

"No, I'll go. I'm moving."

"I don't make the rules, Twelve. I just enforce them."

As we set off toward the warden's office there are two other early risers. Doors slam and female voices argue, growing louder as we near the next cell block. It's a long walk to the office in the company of panic-stricken cries and anti-social jeers from other inmates on the floors beneath, so I drown out their torment with a more useful thought: what use to Titan is banishment anyway? In today's society, hanging would be more efficient and less of a risk to Titan's security. The world outside is dangerous enough without returning, revenge-fuelled citizens.

The current state of *Ad Infinitum* was the fault of a meteor named NORA. It hit Earth in the year 2022 with such force the rotation of our little blue planet gradually came to a stop, plunging half our population into complete darkness for six of the twelve months. That was six hundred and thirty-two years ago when technology was so advanced mankind had some (if limited) ability to prepare for impact. A young engineer named Joseph Czar and his family built our underground ark, Titan. Before the planet succumbed to complete chaos, those deemed valuable- including my ancestors- took refuge here and have remained underground ever since.

An entire civilisation was disjointed within a single generation, divided into the practical and the worthless. It was the latter who remained on the outside during impact. Their ancestors are now Titan's biggest threat. I've always thought that perhaps they wouldn't be if it wasn't for what followed. Leaking nuclear and medical waste from abandoned factories, wars and natural disasters created irradiated food that led to poison and malnutrition. Panic-prompted looting, the destruction of family homes and an increase in severe crime forced survivors to form gangs. These people all followed merciless power-happy warlords, some of whom were later driven insane. The sudden increase in earthquakes, flooding and other natural disasters made finding a safe, permanent shelter impossible. Combined, these events caused millions of horrific deaths and almost wiped any trace of civilisation off the face of the Earth.

Anybody left outside who was not obliterated by NORA, was dead or severely sick before the dust settled and we, safe within Titan, were trapped here for good.

At first, we were ungoverned and disorganised, so the council made the decision to appoint a powerful leader; a saviour amidst the pandemonium. He was the son of Titan's designer. His name was Agaue Czar.

Like most disappointing leaders, Czar had no interest in saving the sick and wounded or in re-populating what remained of Earth. Instead of allowing nature to take its course and humanely dispose of their remains, he banished them to the wasteland. Their much-needed skills, experience and contribution was deemed irrelevant no matter their role. Doctors, engineers and biologists, even if only sick from the common cold, now feared for their lives.

In the year 2654, his descendant Daemon Czar rules in his place, making most of the same mistakes.

"Stop dragging your feet, Twelve," says the guard. I jump from my mental anecdote to find I'm staring at Warden's office door. "Hands up please, fingers spread wide."

I raise my palms to waist height. Chains are secured around my wrists and ankles before we proceed. On approach to the door, another two women appear from the entrance to a neighbouring block.

The first and tallest woman I recognise as inmate Eighteen, making her six inmates more dangerous than I, which is an achievement. Her fine black hair is plaited and she has a strong, soldier's physique. Sweat pours from her forehead and drips between her breasts, indicating she's put up more of a fight that I. Her teeth are clenched, as are her fists, and mud brown eyes study me with urgency.

The other girl is spiritless and frail. I don't know her name or her number, but ocean blue eyes cower behind her raised hands and she sniffles beneath a forest of knotted blonde hair. She's younger; probably in early adolescence. I wonder what she could possibly have done to deserve this.

"Stand straight," my guard tells me. "Warden will be out soon."

"Can you loosen the chains just a bit? I can't go anywhere when you have the keys."

Eighteen grins and rattles her cuffs in protest. Her guard slams the inmate's face against the stone wall, which painfully rebounds into the hold of the warden. After examining her wound with pride and amusement he hands Eighteen back to the guard, then clunks the door closed behind him.

"Sorry for the noise, Sir," says the guard. "This week's selection is feistier than expected."

Warden waves off her apology and because I'm closer than the blonde, he approaches me first. His fingers stroke through my hair. Although I have naturally black hair, in this light it looks duller than ever and is greasy between his chubby fingers.

Warden's breath smells of mint where he's tried to cover the underlying scent of wine and I try not to breathe in his second-hand, alcohol-polluted air. His grey suit is pristine but I notice his hair is ruffled and crease lines decorate one cheek, indicating he's been sleeping at his desk, perhaps following drink.

Aeon Infinitum: Run For Your Life

"Twelve, are you causing trouble? This week's selection is painful; three girls from my first twenty. Looks like some lucky inmates are about to be demoted. It's such a pity to lose you though. What a challenge we've faced trying to control your tempers, particularly Eighteen. Now standing before the face of death you are so feeble and, what's the word?" He presses his lips against my neck and grins. "Oh right, *defenceless*."

"Banishing us won't save this place," Eighteen tells him despite her earlier beating. "We're not sick; we can't infect the ark."

Warden nods. "I agree you're fine specimens physically but mentally you're deranged criminals and Czar demands order."

"I *know* you don't think his methods of disposal are humane, Warden," I say.

"Would you rather I re-instate your full sentence?"

Our eyes meet; my disappointed green to his infuriated brown but I hold my gaze and soon his anger deflates. He releases me without further resistance, then stumbles backwards. The others don't seem to notice he's still intoxicated.

"You're always too vocal, Twelve. I fear this time the price for your mouth may be your life."

"This time perhaps you'll let me pay it."

The warden's fist meets my jaw, knocking me off my feet. Face first I hit the ground and groan in agony until my guard reaches down for me, but spares no sympathy. Furious and embarrassed, Warden gives me a strong kick in the ribs before I can take the guard's hand.

"I need no justification to kill you; remember that I *saved* you, Twelve. In return, I think respect and loyalty are fair. Consider your banishment a lenient punishment for your crime."

"Loyal isn't how *I'd* describe my feelings," says Eighteen, catching my gaze. "How about molested, enslaved, tortured and abused? I could go on. What do *you* think, Twelve?"

It takes all my self-discipline not to laugh. Instead, I spit my loose tooth at the Warden's feet, spraying blood and saliva across the bottom of his trousers. Warden gestures at my guard who lifts me up and launches my body through his office door and into a wooden filing cabinet. I'm completely humiliated but deem the damage to my self-esteem worth the shot at Warden's image. As I breathe through my recovery, Warden sits the blonde inmate behind his desk and hands her a cup of water. Both Eighteen and I narrow our eyes.

"Four, my little Chastity, is such a humble, apologetic thief. Now she knows it's unwise to steal from the kitchens and rations are in place for a reason."

"You call that humble? I call it violated," says Eighteen.

"Let's not label it," says Warden. "My point is you could both learn so much from her. Four takes her fair punishment, following her fair trial, with dignity. I'm almost sorry to have to banish her. She sets an ideal example."

Four, whose name must be Chastity, flinches with every word and avoids any eye contact. She takes a nervous sip and replaces the cup on a coaster, laying her unchained hands in her lap. Warden has her well trained. I have no doubt he's applied varying methods of torture to achieve such results.

"Guards you may wait outside," says Warden. "I doubt we'll have further resistance."

When the guards leave I gesture at the young inmate and raise an eyebrow. "What do you want, Warden? Business? *Pleasure?*"

Warden raises his fist to strike me until he sees Chastity flinch. She turns her head as not to witness the violence and for a fraction of a second, the expression on Warden's stern face is priceless.

"Allegiance sickens me. Once outside these women will be your enemy, Chastity. You'll be praying for those *creatures* to devour them instead and, notably, so will I. These two have given me nothing but trouble in two very different ways."

I interrupt, "Is there a point to this or are you in the business of frightening little girls for fun?"

Eighteen shakes her head. "It's obvious why this kid is so obedient. I'd say it's got something to do with his love of alcohol and women, sometimes together. Right, Warden?"

Warden seizes Eighteen by the throat. "Let me give you some advice. Should you find yourself cornered, alone, injured or lost, perhaps even pinned by a predator, just take your own life because you'll be doing everyone a favour. That's if I don't kill you myself first and believe me I'm tempted."

I reach out and take Chastity's hand whilst Warden is pre-occupied. I lead her from the desk to the door.

"You're a coward." Once I've regained his attention, I continue. "It's a shame because once you were so such a strong-willed, together leader. Now you're, *hmm*, what's the word?" I lightly place my palm on his shoulder until he turns, leaving Eighteen to duck beneath his arm and out of the firing line. "Oh, that's right, *defenceless*."

Scowling, Warden shouts for his guards and they re-enter with their batons drawn. I note they now carry the newer models and assume it's protocol when in the presence of the prison Warden. Sneaking a glance at one of them, they appear to be thicker glowing rods, electric blue in colour. Eighteen's guard draws hers and slams it against her palm for effect, causing a sound like the crack of thunder.

Warden sees I have hold of Four's hand. "On my authority, you will kill this inmate."

"Be careful, Warden. If they find my body within Titan's walls, *Ad Infinitum's* governor will find you. Wouldn't want to end up someone's cellmate now, *would you*?"

Eighteen's guard slips between us and grabs a tight hold of both Four and me together, then drags us out of the office by our sleeves. Once in the corridor, she steers Eighteen after us. I clench my free fist until Warden breaks eye contact and slams the door behind us for effect.

We pause in a brief silence until Warden destroys his office in fury. My guard scowls, so I hold up my wrists voluntarily for my cuffs to be tightened.

"I leave you for *five minutes*, Twelve. You're not helping yourself."

I shrug. "I'm not trying to. I already know I'm screwed. May as well have some fun on the way out."

From the office, we are taken to the food hall where there are dirty dishes and cutlery abandoned on most of the wooden tables. I notice every tin cup is empty and each plate scraped clean; rations haven't been high enough recently and people with physical roles in Titan are surely starving, eating whatever scraps they can get.

"I appreciate what you did but I don't need your help," Four tells me as the guard unlocks her cuffs.

"I beg your pardon? How old are you, kid?"

Four straightens with pride. "I'll be fifteen in two weeks."

"Well, that's unfortunate because you'll be dead by then."

My guard unlocks my restraints so I lower my aching body to a bench.

"I didn't defy Warden to protect you," I explain. "What he said is right; when you're up top you're easy game."

Amused, the guards leave our small party alone to eat. Armed attendants bring us a late meal under Warden's orders and after my helping of porridge, I'm satisfied. Eighteen hands me a cup of water and motions toward Four who is sulking at the next table.

"She doesn't look so good. How's your face?"

"Fine. Tooth has been loose for a while." I shake my head when I catch Chastity staring at me. "I saw how they looked at one another. Do you think he feels any guilt?"

"Banishing her is crueller than the death sentence. At least in here, it's a predictable, swift snap of the neck. Out there who knows? They've spent a lot of time together though so I could be wrong. After all, Warden doesn't select inmates for banishment, he just prepares them."

"He certainly can't love her. Not in prison. Such an emotion is impossible even when you're fourteen and Warden is promising you a comfortable sentence," I reply.

"Nothing about prison is easy," Eighteen says. "Whether you're Warden's favourite or not."

"She's likely spent more time in his bed than in her cell, you know. He's twenty-something and Czar's legal sex age is-"

"You can stop. I can't bear the thought," says Eighteen.

"I'm not wrong though. She's not strong enough to survive out there even alongside us. Those things will obliterate her. Likely all of us, eventually."

"I heard all she did was steal a loaf of bread. Her punishment should be bed without supper." Eighteen pauses then says, "I'm sorry, I never asked your name. I'm the replacement for the woman they hung last week. My name's Corrina."

I accept her handshake. "Eden. What did you do to earn a promotion?"

She drops her head and wrings her fingers together as though I'm in any place to judge. She can't have more blood on her hands than I do.

"Three weeks in isolation, squatting in a bucket, eating with your hands and sleeping on the floor threatens your sanity. My guard came in to feed me and I tried to strangle her."

"With what?"

She holds up her hands. "I'm not proud."

"You're either really brave or really stupid," I reply through stifled laughter, and Eighteen's face softens.

Aeon Infinitum: Run For Your Life

"Though I'd have done the same."

"You're *the* Eden, aren't you?" she says. "I heard what you did. I can't believe you're still alive. There are rumours about you and Warden. Are they true?"

"Probably." I tap my head. "And I'm alive because he can't break me. We're *old friends*. That's all you need to know."

"But you tried to kill Czar! Why not Warden too? I heard he rescued you from immediate execution and delayed your sentence. Is that true? Why did he help you? I'm not sure he did you any favours."

"He didn't, though we're of an opposite opinion. Banishment is Warden's way to kill me without actually having to do so himself. I know you said he has no say in the selection but this time I'm not so sure. If he hangs me he has to watch and he's too much of a coward for that. He's been to Czar, I know it."

Eighteen nods. "Maybe. I'm only in here because a guard overheard me disagree with Czar. She's had it in for me since I reported her for threatening my sister. All she did was run in the corridor by our living quarters. She was late for school and the guard wanted her caned. Anyway, I was telling my friend Liza that I didn't think Czar cared about re-population or the regeneration of Earth because he's too busy recruiting us to explore and protect *this* place. Why can't he see that perfection isn't the answer? For that, I was deemed a threat to society and locked away for treason."

"Let me guess, they gave you the option to Venture?" When Eighteen doesn't reply, I say, "Venturers should be volunteers, not slaves, and certainly not *children*. Banishment is an irreversible way of making you a Venturer. Four is too young to understand the politics. It's better that way, I think."

Eighteen takes a bite of an apple and deep in thought she says, "Why banish *us*? My sentence date was set, yours a life imprisonment unless you re-offend behind bars and Chastity's crime barely worth punishment at all."

"Like I said, Warden is more involved than he'll admit. Czar banishes people because he fears illness, disability, difference in personality and in my opinion, anti-social behaviour, homosexuality, freedom of speech and anything else he doesn't understand. Like the ruling Czar before him, he's probably a criminal himself and banishes anyone he thinks could challenge our leadership. Warden's the same. What he's doing to Chastity needs covering up. If Czar finds out, Warden is at risk of banishment too."

"Getting rid of the evidence then, you suppose?" she asks, eyebrows raised. "If he's molesting her, anyone in this block could have been a witness."

"Oh he's molesting her, I guarantee it. Four is smarter than she looks; it's an awful experience but allowing it has kept her alive and reasonably safe so far."

Eighteen lowers her voice. "He's tried it with you before?"

"Once. He rarely tries now because I broke his nose."

"That was *you*? I remember how foul his temper had been. About a month ago, right?"

I sigh and swallow the rest of my water, then slam the cup down harder than I should, disgusted that Warden has managed to wriggle his way into the only decent conversation at the breakfast table I've had in almost six months.

"Warden obviously regrets saving my life. He's banishing me to resolve that problem and is perhaps using the kid as a means to move on."

"Move on from *what*?" Eighteen asks. "Did you report him after you broke his nose?"

"No, and our past is irrelevant. Better forgotten. Let the kid love him; maybe he'll save her and prove me wrong, but I've cast my vote. Either way, she's got to learn to play his weaknesses. Banishment or not, she's dead anyway."

Eighteen shuffles along the bench and glances back at Four. Warden enters the food hall, ignores our bench, and wraps an arm around the blonde's shoulder. At this, Eighteen scowls and cracks her knuckles.

"Hope you're hungry, girls, I know I am."

Four allows the warden to lead her back to the office. Her entire body is quaking. They try not to stare, but even our guards silence in awe. I too find I've stopped chewing.

"Is it true they prepare you for banishment with training?" Eighteen says when they are out of sight. "She could sure use it."

"Yes but it won't be enough," I say. "Can't teach human nature. Anyway, I'm about done here."

I'm suddenly furious with myself for being too friendly. I might need to kill this woman when the toxins have driven her insane and starvation has convinced her I'm food. Although I'm hoping to avoid killing any familiar faces, I'll do what's necessary to survive. *Nothing* should get in the way of a future free of Titan.

Any hesitation, however brief, will get me slaughtered.

Eighteen grabs my arm and startles me. "We could escape; help get the kid away from Warden. If you want my help-"

"I don't, and you shouldn't be asking."

Eighteen nods and leaves the table, snatching a bread roll and banana to take with her. It's clear I've lowered her expectations when her parting line is, "See you in training, Twelve."

Staff are scurrying to clean and prepare for the next sitting, so I gather the remaining scraps and conceal them in my one-piece prison outfit before following Eighteen through the archway and back toward the Warden's office. A patrolling guard intercepts and escorts me up a flight of stairs for what Warden refers to as FFT– *Friendly Fire Training*- which we'll all ignore.

There are far worse things heading our way than Daemon Czar's terrible leadership and if Warden plans to survive their arrival, banishing me will be the biggest mistake he ever makes. Knowing he'll do so without further consideration, I climb the winding staircase to my first training session with a smile on my face.

2

Elvandra Rae

I'm staring at a tilted stack of inmate records with little enthusiasm. My right hand reaches for a tin cup of cold black coffee; despite it being cold, this action is all I can muster as a distraction from the over-due task I face.

Beside me is my mentor. He's a bald-headed adolescent wearing black satin robes and a continual frown. His name is Veil, which is no surprise because like his name he gives little away. If I shuffle or sigh, he grunts. It's *all* I can hear.

"If you are not going to drink that, Elvandra, I suggest you cease fumbling with it."

"I can't concentrate," I tell him, glancing at the next table and shoving aside the cup of coffee. "They're doing so much better than we are."

"Pay no attention to your colleagues," he replies, and although the order is aimed at me his eyes never leave the document he's reading. "They are already making three severe mistakes. Back to work."

I grin at their overuse of unnatural shades and turn my attention to the table. I ignore the floating fabrics and reflective materials and gesture at an old ink-splattered parchment holding the outline of a female figure. Veil slides the document across the desk toward me. My stomach churns but I'm comforted by my memory's capacity; I've done this before. I can do it again.

"Designing suitable attire demands trial and error we have no time for, Elvandra. We are already late submitting our designs." Veil slams his fist down. His voice deepens; becomes stricter. "Are you listening? We must finish today. Work faster. What have you come up with?"

"Don't rush me, Veil. This shit takes time. I can't work under the pressure and in my defence, I've submitted eight others, all of which *you* rejected."

"This *shit* is your job, Elvandra."

"Then let me do it properly."

I lift a brush to the pallet. Veil crushes leaves and flowers with his knuckles and mixes them with water, then settles to watch me paint. I flick my wrist across the parchment. If I mess up, a young woman will die an agonising death.

"I think they are being too bold," I tell him, leaning over the table and lowering my voice. "Here, see?"

He moves in, weary of our proximity. Veil, I soon learned, doesn't understand intimacy and unlike most humans he doesn't crave it either. I have always been wary of him.

"Camouflage is not their base so we can use the idea without being accused of theft. We need subtle forest shades; materials that breathe and cool but won't snag. Lightweight and flexible but thick enough to protect against sharp objects."

"Like claws," he says with an emotionless expression.

Aeon Infinitum: Run For Your Life

"Yes." I swallow hard. "Like claws or teeth."

"Can you finish within the hour, Elvandra?"

"It's been ten years since my last input, Veil, but I remember this stuff as though it was yesterday. You'll have your design soon. Is a bit of trust too much to ask?"

Veil smirks and gestures at the parchment. "Please, continue."

Banishment roles become available once a month and each time the posts to fill are displayed on the canteen notice board, with perks as payment such as food or tokens. I couldn't refuse the offer of a position here no matter how strongly I disagree with banishment. Czar calls it Justice. I call it murder.

Veil lifts his head and widens his perusing eyes. I pass him the crumpled parchment covered in wet paint and twiddle my thumbs.

"Yes, I think you may have something," he pauses, "Very good. Wait here, Elvandra."

Veil leaves the table and adjusts his hood. Its vicious point brings what would otherwise be a beautiful robe to a domineering finish and most importantly hides his scars. My colleagues all avoid him but it's a fashion statement I can appreciate here in Titan. Better to be left alone to one's thoughts; the more invisible you are, the longer you seem to live.

Pleased to have an unscheduled break, I slump over the desk and trace the shape of a female body with my index finger. I think about this poor girl's chances of survival and my pulse quickens. All I know is her age and her crime.

Although I opted to work here of my own accord (*admittedly for the valuable tokens we use in Titan for laundry, rations and luxuries*), some of the other volunteers haven't considered how their designs might actually get somebody killed. After all the hard work, it's the warden who selects the winner so the majority of my colleagues have been convinced they are detached from any guilt.

While other temporary roles teach wasteland survival skills such as hunting, using tools, making weapons, hand-to-hand combat and sport, the burden is on *our* shoulders to keep banished inmates comfortable and hopefully invisible. Our department is called Wardrobe.

"You got my condolences girl," says an unfamiliar voice from the next table. "Name's Mika. Pleased to meet you."

I swing my legs free from the bench and take the opportunity to stretch. Mika is a stocky woman with long red hair and almond skin. Crimson material hugs each womanly curve and outlines a growing bump. I shake her hand as not to be rude.

"I'm Elvandra. This is *not* an ideal environment for you."

"It's dark but the least strenuous. I'm covering for someone selected for jury duty," she replies, "so I'll be gone by the end of this week anyway." Mika gestures at Veil and cringes. "Damn, he's as odd as they come."

I nod. "Veil's a survivor. Three years ago Czar called for a ten man line up due to an overflowing prison. He was thirteen at the time and was taken from death row. Czar sentenced the men to work outside the grounds. There was a security breach and Veil wound up in the wild. Wardrobe saved his life."

Aeon Infinitum: Run For Your Life

"Besides the robes he doesn't *look* like a criminal. What did he do?"

"I never asked, but do *any* of the banished inmates look so bad these days? My guess is theft though. The banishment was supposed to be temporary and guarded. When he returned, Czar quarantined him for weeks before assigning him to Wardrobe. His death sentence was overturned."

Mika's attention strays. Her eyes fixate on her painting; no pockets, protection or camouflage. It looks nothing like mine. I'd heard from Veil that the line up this month was only three females to one male. Mika's is designed for another woman who is both older and more dangerous than mine.

"Given the circumstances I'm not surprised Czar has called to activate the Harmony Grid," Mika says. "Did Veil tell you what that's about?"

"Not yet but I'm no fool," I say, lowering my voice. "Everyone knows the ark is short of supplies. Banishment won't be a punishment soon, it'll be a means to survive. Do you remember when being banished was only for the terminally ill? Now *everyone* fears it. A part of me still thinks the Harmony Grid is a myth between Venturers though. *Something* is heading our way and opening the doors now to evict more Titans would be suicide for the entire ark. It doesn't make much sense to activate it yet. Don't you agree?"

"It's got *my* attention, myth or not." Mika shudders. "Hate to think what happens then, though, if you're right that is. What if the gates open and we let in more than we let out?"

"Guaranteed extinction, I assure you."

She sighs. "Does your friend know anything?"

This time, Mika nods toward the darkest corner. Across the room my friend Donar is completely hypnotised by his scroll; he hasn't left the bench for refreshments in his entire eight-hour shift. Ever since he learned his prisoner is a fourteen-year-old child locked up for petty theft, he's been obsessed.

"He looks lonely and enraged," Mika says, running her palm gently across her stomach.

"He's neither," I say. "He just hates this place."

I can't blame him. They gave Donar a volunteer mentor named Juliette rather than a past survivor like Veil, so his chances of winning those extra tokens are slim to none. Our colleagues Mika and a woman I haven't yet spoken with named Rose were allotted terrain experts, giving them the advantage. Lucia and Gregor Ivandras are not only husband and wife but are Titan's leading biological researchers. They have ventured themselves several times and have yet to be injured enough to quarantine them. Donar has deemed the rest of us defeated.

"I should see how he's getting on."

I excuse myself and heave a sigh of relief when I'm closer to Donar than to Mika, shuddering as Veil's critical eyes follow. It's easier to ignore his malfunctioning social skills than to challenge them. I try not to glance his way as I slide in beside my colleague and tell him to take a break.

Without glancing up he says, "I haven't even started."

His mentor offers a weak smile as thanks for my efforts and stands. She and Veil chat about the Harmony

Aeon Infinitum: Run For Your Life

Grid, leaving Donar and me alone to exchange pleasantries.

"Finished yet?" he asks.

"Hmm, I think so. Obviously, you're far more dedicated than Veil and I to still be painting on the final day."

"Didn't have much of a choice," says Donar, "damn horse hair won't hold long enough to paint one stroke and it's so bloody dark in here I'm surprised any of us can function. My tools are all old and broken and Juliette has rejected most of my suggestions."

Donar sweeps a frustrated arm across his workspace. Brushes and pots scatter sending an echo across the room. Mika taps Gregor on the arm and points at the chaos. Veil shakes his head.

Embarrassed, I shush Donar and clean up the mess.

"If they weren't broken before they are now," I say. "My eyes are strained too, but the other table has a pregnant temp. Imagine how *she* feels. We all have families to support and those tokens could pull us out of poverty. Bite your tongue and don't blow this, Donar. It's worth the few weeks of torture, then you can go back to the kitchens where you're comfortable."

"Blow this for *who*, Elvandra?"

"Both of us. We agreed to share no matter who wins."

Donar buffs out his chest and impersonates the fat administrator who has been overlooking the operation this month.

"Do you remember what they said? 'So long as Warden deems your design most suitable to support life, you shall be granted twenty-eight days of additional tokens. Is that not all the incentive you need?' The whole system sickens me. Innocent people die for a bit of extra food. Don't tell me to suck it up, Elvandra, because I just can't. I'm ashamed of myself; of *us*."

"Donar, I didn't mean-"

"I signed up for Rehabilitation and missed the cut. At least you can do some good before you send them on their way and give them some pleasant memories of this hell hole."

"Donar, I can't agree."

Rehabilitation would only distract Donar. There's too much pressure on the counsellors to adjust the prisoner's behaviour enough to keep them alive. It's an impossible task at the best of times. He's forgetting most of the poor souls they dump outside Titan's perimeter are convicted criminals, very few of whom pour out their hearts to someone who still calls Titan home. They disagree with the way things are governed and they fear speaking out will only worsen the punishment. Many die as a result of arrogance rather than wounds.

"I'd blame myself if anything happened to one of my own. More people are banished than hung nowadays so the wasteland must be filled with warlords and murderers," I tell him. "I couldn't work in Rehab. Nor could you."

Only now as my eyes adjust to the dim candlelight of the desk do I notice the greying of Donar's hair and darkened circles beneath his emerald eyes. These past few months have aged him and I doubt he has the patience to accommodate failure.

"Their life is in your hands, Donar. More so in Rehab than Wardrobe. Be pleased that part isn't your responsibility."

Donar sighs. "I think I'll take that break now."

Moments later Veil seizes me with a firm grip and drags me to my desk. In the three weeks we've been student and mentor I've never seen him smile. I don't think I ever will.

"Get back to work. I would like our initial design finished by the end of the day."

Day. Here in Titan, we haven't seen the sun in two and a half months. Since NORA started all this, darkness consumes both day and night for half our year. It's devastating for the ecosystem (*and for my sanity*). There is a short period between the two when the temperature is stable and the light is ideal. Before you know it though, you're back to either a scorching desert or several meters of solid snow.

"Isn't the design I gave you good enough?" I ask.

"Your painting is being scrutinised by Needle and Thread. If they can sew it we can finish up. Now leave your colleague alone. Juliette advises they are behind schedule," Veil says. "Donar needs no reminder of why he is here."

"*Food* is the reason he's here. One neither of us are proud of."

I pick up my paintbrush, applying too much green to a blank female outline and transforming it into a tree rather than the expected statement of power and ability. Czar encourages all departments to reflect *Ad Infinitum's* four core statements which have always been balance, belief, obedience and just. In Wardrobe, we must display them somewhere visible on our designs, so my usual method is to scribble the words along the sleeve. Oh and

Czar's motto, too: *Ad Infinitum: your promises kept.*

After my conversation with Donar I use red paint to write the motto across the chest, as if in blood, then splash the rest across the image out of boredom. Veil grabs my wrist and the crook of his mouth upturns. For a moment I think he'll manage a smile.

"Take the rest of the day off."

"But you just said-"

"I know what I said. I'm going to overrule Needle and Thread's judgement."

"You can't be serious?" I stare at the khaki splodge. "You want to dress this girl as a treasonous mound of mud? I was only-"

"Being stubborn and doodling, yes I know."

Veil rolls the parchment and conceals it in his robes. He growls, forcing a nosey Mika to concentrate on her own work.

"Your presence is no longer required in Wardrobe. Get some rest. You look like you could use it."

Veils advice, however out of character, is worth taking. I gather my equipment and stagger blindly beneath the archway in the poor lighting that leads to the draughty stone corridor of Sector W. Lower temperatures are normal for the time of year within Titan. It may be cold here but it's freezing on levels closer to the surface. Most of those inhabitants are evacuated to units that were originally built as bomb shelters. They haven't been used for that purpose in hundreds of years though.

Titan's first inhabitants will have used those units during the impact of NORA. It hit us so hard that twenty-five percent of Earth's population died instantly

Aeon Infinitum: Run For Your Life

and another five percent were severely injured and dead before the month's end. Forty percent were mutated or sick because of the after effects and another fifteen driven insane. They lost so much so suddenly. The remaining fifteen percent survived in a bunker like ours, though we're not aware of another for at least fifty miles in any direction. We still have hope, though.

By now I've memorised how to move promptly and with ease through the inscribed, dome-shaped tunnels which form a labyrinth of underground offices and facilities for Wardrobe workers in Sector W. Trembling from the cold I pick up the pace, passing a couple of supervisory allotments before reaching my own, which I share with Donar. It has a small living room with a tatty grey rug, furnished with the basics. The walls and floors are bare stone with no windows, but it's safe and dry, so I'm grateful.

A wash and change of clothes are first on my mind. Once in my bedroom, I strip to my undergarments. Wrinkles decorate the nooks of my eyes and my skin is pale and lifeless. Hazel locks wave to my shoulders and my bottle green eyes are failing. I avoid my reflection in the mirror. I don't need to be reminded of how awful I look for a twenty-five-year-old.

This place is familiar because I've bunked here before. Ten years ago I dressed a brave boy of seventeen who required clothing fit to hold heavy research equipment. Woven into the jacket were straps, belts and pockets for food and tools, freeing the boy's hands to fight - a very important requirement. Only when his hunting skills failed did he die of starvation.

I scrub my face and hands a little harder than I

should as if to banish the haunting memory and jump when the door to our dorm creaks open. I slip into my gown and meet Donar in the living room.

"Juliette released you," I say, lighting the nearest candle. "Did you finish?"

"For today I'm done with Wardrobe banter." Donar runs paint covered hands through his hair and sighs. "Listen, about earlier-"

"No apology needed. The job has erased my manners and we're on the same team, even if technically we can't be."

Only a week ago I found out one of last year's prisoners was Donar's brother, Pagen. Since he told me I've tried to be lenient with his temper. He has more than ten years on me and although we've only shared a home for a few weeks, already he's like family. In the main hall where we eat, paint and were initially briefed, Wardrobe workers are isolated to their designated workspace and too much time with your stern-faced mentor can drive you berserk. With a past as painful as Donar's, when we retire to our dorm it's our opportunity to discuss something lighter. Today though, Donar is willing to talk about our situation more than usual.

"I want to win those tokens more than anything. I can finally support my family. I forgot to ask you, how is your sister?"

"Flona's *working*. Czar only hates the lower class when he's not using them for sex. I keep telling her prostitution isn't the answer but it pays better than selling our herbal remedies. She hates that I'm working for Wardrobe now but if it keeps us alive and out of prison, I'm willing. I read about your father by the way.

I'm sorry, Donar. Why didn't you tell me?"

"He was lucky to reach eighty. Pagen's banishment ruined him and a broken ticker kills the strongest of men."

Each word is an unintentionally spiteful curse on Czar and all he rules. Under his orders the guards control every prison, hospital and kitchen in what remains of the ark, so Donar lowers his voice every time Titan's laws are our topic for conversation.

"Pagen's friends bet highly on his survival you know; his strong muscular and skeletal structure, height, build and natural hunting skills named him most likely to live that month." Donar releases me and slumps down on one of the chairs. "How did you find out about my father?"

"I like to know who lies in the bed beside me. Research is good sense. You know me, I'm nosey."

He smiles and gestures at the door. "You bribed the night guard again?"

"Ah, that guy will break for an extra ration of bread any day. I don't mean to pry but I saw the infirmary's stamp on the letter and it worried me. Are you mad?"

"No," he says, smiling. "It's nice that you care."

I kiss Donar on the forehead. "I care that we're being shown the Harmony Grid plans tomorrow too. It'll be an awkward day so we should get some rest."

"Sounds like a good idea," he says.

I retire to my room and lay beneath the sheets in silence. The labyrinth is tranquil as our colleagues settle for tomorrow's bedlam. I close my eyes and savour a peaceful slumber for the final time.

3

Elvandra Rae

Wardrobe is woken early to the boom of the breakfast gong. Although I'm well rested, I'm beginning to experience the effects of a deeply routed migraine whereby my vision has been interrupted by jagged yellow lines and my face feels tender down the right hand side. I tug on a dusty cream dress and join Donar in the dorm to await an escort to the Harmony Grid briefing.

"What's wrong, Elvandra?" he asks as he gently twirls me. He fumbles with a piece of string to knot my brown hair in a high bun. "Did you sleep well?"

"I slept fine but working in the dark isn't good for us. I can't do this much longer. My head hurts."

Donar loosens the bun and smiles. "You won't have to for much longer, but I can speak with Veil if you want to skip the briefing. I'll bring back my notes for you and we can discuss the Harmony Grid later."

"I need to hear this for myself," I say, smiling, "but I appreciate the offer. We'll be out before lunch. I can sleep then."

Ten minutes later a guard knocks on the door and calls our names. He motions us out of the dorm and together we begin our brief walk to Wardrobe's main hall.

Benches form the meeting's seating area and replace our painting tables, which have been temporarily stacked at the far end of the room. When the last worker has been seated, we're joined by a heavyset cartographer with mouse-brown hair and a moustache, dressed from head to foot in black. He stands at the front beside a cork board but instead of addressing us, we are welcomed by his female companion; a tall blonde in a navy dress. I wonder if he's mute or just shy.

"I've taken the time to study your initial designs," she says. "I must congratulate the mentors. Their work has paid off."

Veil grunts and elbows me in the ribs for yawning but I'm within my rights. Our success is not only because of their advice. Veil may have more field experience than I, but he will *never* match my skills in haberdashery.

"I'm here to tell you about the Harmony Grid," she continues.

I raise my hand and speak out of turn. "Excuse me, can we presume Titan *is* dying then?"

Donar cringes and nudges me. Through grinding teeth he asks, "Are you crazy?"

"Somebody had to ask. We're all thinking it," I reply, loud enough for her to hear me.

Without answering, the cartographer pins gold stars on his map, identifying the exits to Titan. Veil rummages in his robes for a sheet of paper and pencil to take notes. Outside our fences, the man pins stars in seven more places. Each location appears to be at least five or six

Aeon Infinitum: Run For Your Life

miles from Titan and the same from each other.

"Who are you?" the woman asks with narrowed eyes.

"I'm Elvandra Rae, a designer for Wardrobe."

"Well Elvandra, my name is Zthora and I don't like to be interrupted, however valid your question is." She gestures at the map. "You are being briefed today because our ark *is* failing to support the ever-growing population. This shouldn't come as a surprise; rations have been low for a while and attacks are persistent."

"Understatement of the year," Mika whispers from the bench behind us.

I snort through stifled laughter, drawing the attention of my colleagues. Zthora pauses as Veil nudges me and abruptly tells me to shut up.

"Our generator and farming facilities have surprised us. When Titan was originally built our ancestors were only expecting to live here for two hundred years until the dust settled. We can ask no more of the ark. It is time we moved on."

Without interrupting, Gregor raises his hand and is prompted by the cartographer. "Do this month's banished inmates know about the Harmony Grid?" he asks. "It seems a pointless punishment if Titan is going to be evacuated anyway."

Zthora nods. "Yes it is and they were briefed earlier. The Harmony Grid is only in place because of Czar's Venturers; those who are paid to explore and return with research. From their work, our cartographer has compiled what you see here." After giving us time to get a better look, she continues. "As you will know, other banished prisoners who have miraculously survived the wasteland are forming a militia and threatening Titan's security. At this time of year, we are under threat from cannibals and various other mutant creatures who have evolved to follow Earth's six months of night. There has been too much damage over the past twelve months to ignore. Czar has decided a team of three Venturers from the Exigency faction should take the next set of banished prisoners across the Harmony Grid to confirm if one particular discovery will make an ideal home."

Zthora gestures at Juliette who has since raised her hand. "If they return with positive results, then what?"

"Czar has authorised an evacuation to a secondary ark, which appears to have been started at the same time as Titan but construction was never completed." Zthora beams at her colleague who taps the seven external stars on the map. "These points mark entrances to the new ark which have already been identified. Is there a question at the back?"

"Yes," says Mika as she lowers her hand. "If and when Titan is evacuated, it would be too dangerous to move in small groups, but it will also draw too much attention if we move as one community. How is Czar going to guarantee our survival?"

Zthora smiles. "Actually Czar can only help the strongest, healthiest and most skilled of you. It will be impossible to move everyone, so he has sentenced Titan to a survival test. With the exception of government personnel, citizens will compete in a race across *Ad Infinitum*'s wasteland to the ark." Zthora scans the audience for questions and finding none, she continues. "We need to strengthen the new ark in line with Titan's current weaknesses," Zthora pauses and sighs, "its

Aeon Infinitum: Run For Your Life

population."

I raise a hand but again speak before I'm asked. "So you knew about this place but waited until now to tell Titan? In doing so *you* have created our problems and yet we're being blamed for making Titan weak."

The tension in Veil's upper body says he's not encouraged by my outburst. Zthora too seems disgruntled.

"We *did* keep the ark a secret but with good reason. We didn't want to lose it to the banished. People leave here on a monthly basis, remember."

I'm not convinced, but when Veil stabs me in the thigh with his pencil I take the hint and settle down. I rub my leg and Zthora continues as though I hadn't challenged her.

"You will be divided into groups based on sectors and factions, so you will not be running with friends from Wardrobe unless you work here permanently."

Mumbles of concern fill the room. It's obvious from the noise that we'd prefer to run with groups of our choosing. We've all built strong relationships in Wardrobe.

"This month's banished inmates will be in FFT for one week before their sentence begins and they will return before the sun rises. If they report good news the evacuation will be imminent. Czar cannot keep the ark open for long, so anyone left outside will be locked outside." Zthora grins because she knows the next part will not apply to her. "It's an old saying but I suggest you remember that you need only run faster than the person behind you."

The cartographer, proving my mute theory wrong,

finishes by explaining the prisoners will have just three months to complete their task before the sun begins to rise. They will encounter new dangers with every step they take, leaving Titan behind to prepare for their own challenges.

No doubt as disgusted as the rest of us, Veil clears his throat and snaps the pencil in two. To my surprise, he then raises a hand and waits until the cartographer points him out.

Veil begins by saying, "Stop me if I am incorrect, but I was under the impression that the Harmony Grid was *not* a guaranteed success. Each star on your map is a proposed place of relative safety."

"That's correct. These are entrances to the new ark. As you can see the perimeter stretches for miles."

"It is not yet proven and not yet inhabited to our knowledge," Veil says. "In reality it is probably overgrown and untouched, perhaps filled with worse dangers unless somebody else has claimed it already, but the world is dead; besides mutants, animals and plant life the existence of survivors *is* unlikely. So tell me, how do you plan to lock people out of an abandoned, unfinished ark; one which you do not own and do not control? Perhaps there is something you are choosing not to tell us?"

"We *don't* know much," the man says, "but this month's banished inmates will discover the state of the Harmony Grid and report back with their findings. Czar has not yet sent people to work on the ark because he wants to know the layout and facilities first. We will review the situation before evacuating."

"That does not answer the question," Veil says.

"How are you going to lock people out of a building you have no control of?"

Zthora inhales, exhausted by our tireless questions and complaints. Czar must not have warned her that his people are smarter than they seem and will be unlikely to trust in an ill-planned operation.

"Czar's men will guard the perimeter until we have the physical means to barricade the entrance from the inside," she says.

"I see." After a short pause, Veil raises his hand again. "May I ask, what will Czar do if individuals he deems useless arrive before his preferred population, or instead of?"

"This is about population control, not favouritism," Zthora says. "Are we done?"

Veil lowers his head. "Yes, that is all the information I need."

The cartographer clasps his hands and rocks on his heels, pausing for several minutes before speaking again. He must not trust Veil not to argue further but whatever the reason, I'm irritated by the delay.

"Czar asks that Wardrobe prepare provisions to protect as many citizens as possible within the next three months. They will need suitable attire for desert terrain. Your usual schedules and jobs have been cancelled. You are to remain here until a decision is made."

I rub my aching head. Another *twelve weeks*?

"So we're forced to spend what may remain of our lives in Wardrobe, but we can't run with anyone here that we care about?" Juliette asks.

I pinch Veil to get his attention and whisper, "This *must* be murder. I'm not suggesting any of us can even make it but do you really want to risk your life, again, for a place that sounds less than adequate, to then work for a man who doesn't even want you there? Can we appeal?"

"The orders to evacuate have not yet been given, Elvandra," he replies. "Until the prisoners return with positive results, we have no power."

"Why, are you expecting the results to be negative?"

Veil ignores me.

Donar rests his head in his hands, defeated.

"How do you feel, Donar, having heard *that*? Let me guess, you've got a terrible headache?"

"It's a Harmony Grid to die for," he says, glancing sideways at our row of Wardrobe workers. "Hey Juliette, can you write me a sick note please?"

"To be excused from what?" she asks.

"Our future." Donar groans and slumps forward, stuffing his head between his knees. "We're all going to die, aren't we?"

***

The next day Donar and I sit opposite one another in our dormitory, waiting for the breakfast gong with nothing sane to say. Yesterday we met the inmates assigned to us and since then Donar has been unusually fidgety. His eyes dart around the room, fingers intertwining and breathing panicked. His fourteen-year-old female turned out to be a blonde thief called Chastity and mine a nineteen-year-old attempted murderer.

All my energy drains when I stand. Neither of us slept, listening to the clangs and distant voices as

Aeon Infinitum: Run For Your Life

Wardrobe made their final overnight preparations. I'm exhausted and impatient but I can't ignore Donar's strange behaviour.

"Everything all right?"

Donar looks away. "Fine."

"I'm sorry you got the kid. If I could switch places I would."

"Her name's Chastity. She's tiny and overly confident; obviously immature. Our efforts won't save her. I'll bet that's why Czar chose banishment; she's an easy victim."

I shrug because we don't know for sure. "I met the Venturers he's sending with them today. They said there aren't any known virus threats at the moment. If she covers up, isn't bitten or scratched then there's every chance she'll survive. Her friends too. Eden's strong and fit but Rehab are sure to have their hands full."

Donar blinks back tears. I take his hand, pull him to my side and embrace him. Body heat encircles us, separating our intimate moment from the hideous truth of this place.

"I *hate* it here," he says. "The Harmony Grid is a myth. Czar's sending people outside to die because he can't feed or control them. This bunch are no different, nor are we. Do you think he has *any* confidence in their return? I don't; in my opinion Czar has no intention of relocating us at all."

Perhaps not but Titan was never supposed to be a permanent fix. Humans were meant to explore once again; our ancestors planned it, prepared and encouraged curiosity. I can't imagine Czar would ignore their legacy.

"If it's real then these are places NORA didn't ruin,"

I reason. "They train Venturers to be resilient and blind to the atrocities. *We* can help to prepare those who aren't as practised for the journey so they're certain to return. What Czar does after that is out of our hands."

"Do you think Eden and Chastity will come back for us?" Donar's grip tightens. "Who could blame them if they kill their mentors and run? Our prison system is cruel and merciless. These sanctuaries could remain undiscovered by Titan forever if that happens."

I reply confidently although on the inside I'm in two minds. The dorm suddenly feels cold, as though my own ghost just strayed right through me. It's a terrifying thought Donar and I share as we shudder in unison.

"Human beings don't abandon one another."

"They will when the running starts," he says, rubbing the goose pimples from his arms. "In such devastating times you'd think the human race might realise we need one another too damn much."

"The world is exciting Donar, but it's a lonely existence without companionship. They won't leave us."

Donar bites his nails as the distant drum of boots sounds at the end of the corridor. The guards are coming for us once again to complete our designs.

"We can't trust anyone now," he says. "I feel so fragile."

"What do you want to do about it?"

Donar says nothing, just shakes his head.

"If those Venturers don't come back Czar will kick every useless human out of Titan to prolong his own life. We'll be outside with no food, water, protection or leadership. If they return with confirmation then Czar will do exactly the same but instead, he'll point us in the direction of safety and wish us luck. There are secrets and lies in operation because he'll survive this whether they return or not." I raise an eyebrow. "Czar takes care of Czar. My point being-"

"-either way we're on our own."

"*We're* alone. Not you. Not I. *We*."

Donar grumbles. "Loyalty isn't your priority, Rae. I'm older, weaker and slower. Without me you'd have a fighting chance."

"If you go, I do too. I'll bet my inmate knows more than she's letting on too. After all, she's in for attempted murder. There's got to be *some* way out of Titan without being noticed. Plenty of abandoned corridors, maintenance rooms and caves. There's a well in Serenity that leads to an underground stream. If we go alone it means abandoning our inmates and could you forgive yourself for perhaps ruining their chance at success?" When Donar shakes his head I say, "Then we befriend them. If we must, we'll just ask nicely. I'll speak to Warden. He and Eden have a history; she might listen to him. They're criminals but they're still human, right? Tomorrow you and I can finish Chastity's clothing together then work on something of our own."

"We can't run, Rae, you have a sister and we both have friends and colleagues."

There's a hammering on the door as I tell him, "Their future might depend on *our* skills so we'll stick this out as long as possible."

"Our future is dark, as is the world. Existing just isn't going to be easy anymore."

Donar opens the door just as the breakfast gong sounds. I find myself laughing when the guard

manhandles me into the corridor.
"Was it ever?"

4

Ginny Bede

My newest client is a sixteen-year-old female and before I've heard her story, I'm already wondering which of our three factions to assign her.

Here in Sector B within the Rehabilitation department, which splits into two miles of tunnels, halls, sleeping quarters and this, our *Gravitās*- a place to discuss politics- it's my job to hire and fire citizens. The *Gravitās* is where all decisions are made and implemented. It's also this client's only hope.

"Rachana, I'm not sure you should be drinking that."

She gulps down her final mouthful of ale. I take her pitcher and slide it across the table out of reach. Instead of protesting she passes out, slumped at an awkward angle between my brother, Mitchell and I.

"Still sure she's Exigency material?" I glance up at Mitchell and sigh, "because I'm not encouraged."

"One hundred percent. Hey, *I* did alright in Exigency." He pats her back even though she probably can't hear him. "Drown your sorrows tonight, Kid. Nobody here will judge you. Besides, the alternative to a faction isn't *so* bad. Another drink?"

I bat away his hand. "She's had enough and I

wouldn't exactly say you turned out great. I'd prefer to assign her to Expediency or Serenity where she won't get hurt. If I can't find her a faction her choices are minimal."

"Ginny, you can't protect them all. Let the assessment figure it out for you in the morning. Until then, drink up."

"This is our meeting hall, not a tavern. I can't discuss her future if she's intoxicated. She's no use to anyone in the wrong faction."

Besides telling her inappropriate jokes, Mitchell has behaved reasonably well until now. After his fourth drink, things tend to go downhill. The pre-arranged approach when he's sober is to share gruesome tales from the wasteland, driving young recruits to go for less strenuous roles around Titan. If they are strong-willed it usually affects the assessment results. It's what I asked him to do before we met Rachana and what he's failed to do so far. Only those who are encouraged by Mitchell's tales instead of being disheartened are considered for Exigency. It's our job in Rehabilitation to take damaged orphans like Rachana and figure out if they are Exigency material. We filter the weak, filter the frightened and filter the warriors so Czar can benefit from their hard work.

Rachana has seemed interested only in forgetting her childhood; in moving forward. Although she hasn't acknowledged her anger when she's awake those amber eyes and clenched jaw prove a longing for revenge.

"Did you get anything out of her, Mitch?"

He nods. "Before you got here she told me Czar hung both her parents for petty crime. Full prisons or something. He couldn't waste resources on keeping criminals alive so they could only re-offend later."

"Does she need a room?" asks Jan.

Jan is one of Mitchell's oldest friends. Her role is in Serenity like mine; we're the back office brains of the Venturing programme. Jan takes care of the temporary accommodation for new recruits.

"Room three has fresh sheets. I don't think anyone has claimed it yet."

"If her parents' quarters have been re-assigned she'll stay with me until a decision regarding her new faction can be made. If the room is still available tomorrow evening I'll book it for her," I reply.

I have always insisted new recruits spend the evening in my dorm so I can fully assess their capabilities. I can't note emotional responses or familiarise myself with personalities from down the corridor. Nobody should be alone on their first evening in Rehab anyway.

"Well there's no better man for the job," Mitchell says, laughing. He slaps me hard on the back. "Gin'll take care of her."

Yawning, I haul an unconscious Rachana over my shoulder, cautious to avoid rousing her sensitive stomach, then say goodnight to those resting in the *Gravitās*. Mitchell staggers off in the direction of the tavern for one more and it'll be the last I see of him no doubt for another twenty-four hours.

This time of year our side of *Ad Infinitum* settles in complete darkness. Candlelight leads the way along a narrow tunnel to my dormitory, passing the latrines and a fresh water well on the way. Feeding it is an underground river. I stop only to fill my canteen for the kid and fasten it to my belt. Each slosh of water and groan from the orphan is a welcome soundtrack in this dead silence.

I use my foot to wedge open the door and my free hand to light a candle. Home is as I left it; quiet and empty. Rachana's weight on my shoulder causes it to ache so I lay her on the moth-eaten sofa and disappear to find us something to eat. Upon my return she's awake and knelt on the floor, trying to light the fire. Occasionally she rubs her forehead and grumbles. I'm startled by her recovery and kneel to help.

"I'm fine," she says.

Wisps of smoke rise from the embers and already the dorm feels warmer. Rachana seats herself on the sofa, tucking thick orange curls behind one ear. I hand her an apple and a blanket which she cradles against her chest, then offer her my canteen.

"Aren't you tired anymore? You had a lot to drink."

"I heal quickly." She takes a sip of water. "Where'd you get so much fruit this time of year?"

I'm not so worried about her telling anyone my trade tricks, only that she'll try my methods of illegal acquirement herself.

"Better you're ignorant. Listen, I owe you an apology. You're too young for this. When I lost my parents, Mitchell gave me his pitcher and said, 'drink up, kid. *Your promises kept*' and I said, 'screw Czar and his promises'. I remember the day well and *you* don't need such memories."

Rachana smiles and gestures with her head at the kitchen where there are empty wine bottles abandoned in the sink.

"You blame your brother for your alcoholism."

I'd forgotten about the mess. I hurry to the kitchen and begin to clear up so I can pretend for thirty seconds that there's a perfectly good explanation. There isn't.

Instead of denying it, I reply, "No I blame myself. I may not be the best company but I've worn your shoes, bought the shirt and waved the flag. It's my job to make sure you don't end up like me. Funny how things work out, huh?"

"A little. If you can fix emptiness I'll be impressed," she says. Her face is pale, eyes mourning. "It's like I have so much emotion that my head can't cope so it's just ignoring it. Is that normal? Anyone else ever reacted this way after losing loved ones?"

I nod because it's true. Lots of orphans I've assessed have expressed the same struggle.

"Hollow is a frequent feeling in this sector, so abandon the drink while you can and ignore my brother's methods of comfort. There are other ways to grieve, though he means well."

Rachana offers half a smile and to kill the awkward silence that has settled upon the dorm, she asks me an unusual question.

"So, what's '*your promises kept*'?"

I'm surprised because nobody has ever had to ask before. It's a question I can answer though. When I sit beside her on the sofa my weight sends choking puffs of dust into the air.

"It's Czar's ideology for a better existence," I say between coughs. "He'll keep his promises if his people keep theirs. I'm stunned by the question. You have to know these things if you're to join Exigency."

"I didn't know there would be a test," she replies. "In fact I had no interest until I saw my father resist arrest when the guards came. No matter what he said it didn't help; Czar had made up his mind before the trial anyway. Witnessing that made me want out of this place even if only temporarily."

"Resistance isn't an option anymore," I tell her, "but he was brave to try. You should still think hard about the faction you want. Lots of kids your age were too eager to join Exigency and prematurely lost their lives."

"You must have been a Venturer once to get a job like this, Ginny. What's it like?"

I pick up the canteen and re-offer her it, unconvinced by the brave face she's putting on.

"I can hide behind my job to some extent now but up there we were *always* in trouble. Death often seems like a blessing these days, soon even more so with the implementation of the Harmony Grid and death is life out there. I'm not sure how much longer I can take this gradual starvation."

Rachana hugs her body as if to shrink her presence.

"I once met a Venturer," she says, "and he said there are others out there like us. Not mutants I mean, but men with functioning senses and intelligence."

"I hope so but there's no solid evidence yet. Most creatures we've photographed are blind or deaf or disfigured somehow. Nuclear fallout does that. They're violent, too. After all these years it's looking bleak, kid."

She scowls. "Are you saying Venturers don't keep secrets? Perhaps they *have* met others but haven't told anyone. Czar could be covering it up. Father thought they'd help overthrow the government and free us if we found them, unless Czar got to them first- other humans that is- offered them something as a bribe to stay hidden. Speculation got my parents killed so there must be *something* behind the story."

I'm uncomfortable handling politics with a sixteen-year-old girl but I'm also pleased she's opening up at such an early stage of the assessment. I merely shrug. Truth is, there are no means to find out what's really going on outside Titan without becoming a Venturer.

"We could end this infinite darkness," Rachana says. Her eyes widen as she stares in deep thought at the fire. "Imagine that."

I'm thrown by her enthusiasm. If Czar or one of his men heard such talk she'd soon be joining her parents.

"Evil as the Czar family has been in the past, the human race *has* survived." I gesture at the apple. "Eat. You need your strength. Look, I'm not saying that your father wasn't courageous to openly discuss Czar's secrets but the darkness will never end, Rachana. A change of leadership won't rewind time. NORA forced this upon us, not Czar. A stationary planet banishes all seasons, all sense of night and day, of temperature, of sanity. I know right now it seems Titan is in a depression but the survivors aren't proven and grasping at the idea will only disappoint. Venturers are expendable and that's the real truth. Czar doesn't care who lives and dies so long as he gets results; the stories are only there to encourage people to join the programme."

"I thought Czar needed Venturers? Why would he hire people just to watch them die?"

"Oh he doesn't but it's a very dangerous job. They

are always running from something rather than toward it. If you really want to be a Venturer then figure out friend from foe now before going out to the wasteland. What remains of old Earth is unpleasant and infectious and if another Venturer can live by sacrificing you, they will. The programme advertises teamwork but when a hungry beast is chasing you, human nature and survival instinct outweigh friendships. Mitchell was supposed to cover all this in the *Gravitās* so I'm sorry you're having to hear it from me. Venturers spend more time fighting than they do researching the wasteland. *There's* your truth."

"Once they're released can't they just disappear? *I* would."

"I can imagine some have been tempted. Titan is equally as unpleasant as the wasteland but for different reasons. Here there is shelter and food, however limited. Out there militia rule most of the land nearby so if Venturers tried to live alone, they'd likely be killed for trespassing. I know it sounds glamorous and free but don't dwell on a myth."

Rachana's cheeks are flushed and her eyes are narrow. She chews rhythmically as she tries to process all I've told her.

Then she asks, "What about the travellers' signs? The guy I met said they leave them all over the wasteland in hope of getting a response. Do you think Czar could be covering something up there?"

Rachana is giving Czar more credit than he's due.

"He and I once Ventured together when he came with our group on a six-month expedition, expecting flowers and woodland creatures." I shake my head at the memory. "He experienced the opposite, much to his dismay. Few people know this, but Czar was actually bitten because he chose to ignore the traveller's signs somebody had left as a warning. One of his own people. We strayed into a den and were attacked. Czar's men had to quarantine him for three days. After that he decided to remain behind a desk and have others do his bidding. If our own won't take note of the signs, how can we expect others to?"

"I guess," she says. "Did the creature have a name?"

"Most names given to the mutants are from fiction books based on likeness and fear. Vampires and zombies, that sort of thing. Our scientists don't know any better and the government won't allow many specimens to enter Titan, dead or alive due to fear of infection and contamination. They name them as they see them."

Czar's men often announce they've discovered something worthy of an autopsy. Most of the time it's to give false reassurance and hope.

"Czar tramples thousands of Venturers across *Ad Infinitum* every year without consideration for the new ecosystem and he wonders why we're at war with the banished. No amount of symbols can resolve the problems he's caused."

Rachana stares at me, her mouth agape.

"Are you're saying the land belongs to the mutants and Czar's Venturers are trespassing? Seems unlikely. They're all barbarians."

"They aren't barbarians. They are people like you and I who were deemed useless. Keep eating or I'll stop talking." Another bite of the apple and I'm back to my lecture. "I'm just saying that Czar has no respect for the creatures who call the wasteland home. Most may not even be dangerous but when threatened, they're bound to protect themselves. Czar believes he can play God and destruction is unfortunately in human nature; most certainly in his. The banished are under the impression, and rightly so, that if they were cast out then Titan must not want the wasteland or see it as a dumping ground, so they've made it their home. This makes perfect sense to you and I but Czar likes to think he can control everything, including the people he technically doesn't want. He's angered a lot of other species because of his arrogance." I sigh. "You should study the signs anyway, so here, if I haven't put you off yet."

I hand Rachana a piece of stained parchment having rummaged through my pockets. Traveller signs can be life-saving and state our intentions to any creatures capable of speech, if they even exist. Venturers have been using them since the first day to leave messages for one another. The deeper Rachana can understand them, the safer she will be if placed in Exigency.

"They're just squiggly symbols," she says, bemused. Her eyes caress each mark with curiosity. "I was expecting more."

"You're not the first to say so. Basic semiotics, that's all. Traveller's signs are our way of saying, 'I was here and now I'm not'. An imprint. A history. A map. Communication to prevent a war nobody wants or needs on either side, if people bother to learn and read them. So many heard my brother explain what I just did and were put off by the idea of Venturing." I motion at her food. "Keep eating."

Rachana nibbles the fruit to the core.

"So you're a teacher then; you train new Venturers

like me to survive outside?"

"Not exactly, we have an entire department for that. *My* job is to guide new recruits and help them understand how dangerous Venturing is. They make up their own minds in the end, though. You could say I'm the man who gets to read your thoughts. I place you in a suitable role where you will be useful and where you can naturally progress through each skill, because Venturers don't just explore, Rachana, they work within Titan. There are three factions. Rehab don't just counsel banished inmates. We counsel volunteers too.

"Venturers are divided depending on skill set so you'll be assigned to one of three. Serenity, my faction, is where we use our heads. We're the back office staff that help to organise and prepare for each expedition. Exigency is Venturing as you know it. They use their fists and their physique to protect this place and gather research. They bring it to us in Serenity for analysis. Or if you're lucky you could be assigned to Expediency; they help Titan by building perimeters and growing food. You get the best of both worlds, really. The freedom of the outdoors with the safety- to some extent- of Serenity."

"Am I staying with you so you can decide?"

"Czar placed me in charge of Rehab because he trusts my judgement. I can read people better than they read themselves. I have *never* placed somebody in a faction that wasn't completely compatible with their personality or their capabilities. Being a part of Rehab reminds me that I'm not doing this for Czar's benefit but for Titan's people."

Rachana frowns. "How do you mean?"

"The last kid who passed through here I assigned to Exigency because of his physical strength, speed and quick wit. You need those things if you're going to survive the wasteland. Because of my decision, Titan have gained a strong soldier who can help protect us. Wouldn't do to stick him in Serenity where those muscles will only wither, right?"

"So you work as per Czar's standards but for Titan's benefit? Sounds as though *you're* running this place, Ginny."

I grin. "You're a smart girl. What do you think so far?"

Rachana picks at the fibres in the blanket. "Unless you place me in Serenity I guess it doesn't matter what I think."

I laugh and point to the bedroom. *Now* she's getting it.

"How long since you slept, alcohol-related unconsciousness aside?"

"A while, but I have too many questions to sleep."

"No more answers until morning then. You take the room, I'll take the couch."

"Wait, what do I have to do to prove I'm Serenity material? I did want to Venture but now I'm not sure. You've kind of scared me." As I stand, Rachana grabs my arm. "I overheard your brother talking about 'taking care' of me. Am I here for business or pleasure?"

Flummoxed, I answer, "Want to entertain lonely alcoholics? Become a prostitute. Now get some sleep. We can talk more in the morning."

We bid one another goodnight to settle in the silence of this everlasting darkness, except I can't drift with a busy brain. I keep thinking about Rachana's suggestion that Venturers could be covering something up. If other humans exist, could they do all she suggested? Would they, given an incentive? If only one sign gained a sane response, then we'd know for sure.

Your promises kept. Czar's glorious slogan for *Ad Infinitum*'s post-NORA government. A reminder that combined we can all contribute to a fresher existence merely by keeping our promises, telling the truth and showing compassion. I used to agree with Czar's methods. Now, I'm only sorry Eden's assassination attempt didn't work out.

My thoughts are with her as I drift off to sleep.

***

The following morning Rachana wakes earlier than expected. Cross-legged she sits by the fire, rocks on her behind and glares at the sofa until my eyes open, startled and forgetful.

I throw back my blanket, scratch my scalp and yawn. Today I'll have to assess our new recruit for Serenity suitability and although Rachana is smart, witty and level-headed, her age and curiosity will lower the likelihood of her being placed here. Already I'm beginning to think she's too frightened for Exigency and too outspoken for Serenity.

"You're not tired? No headache or sickness?"

"I told you, I heal quickly," she replies.

"Emotionally?"

I pause, studying her eyes as they lower. It's clear she's lost some sleep to her parents' memory.

"I'm fine, honest."

"You shouldn't struggle in silence, Rachana, especially not today. Serenity needs to see your intelligence. It's not about fighting back tears; sadness is normal and healthy and Serenity knows that. It's all part of working in Rehab."

Rachana nods, eager to begin the day. "I'm ready, Ginny. Do your worst."

5

Eden Maas

Friendly fire is far too tempting.

During training, I'm joined by the other inmates and soon they'll be potential foes (if they aren't already). We've been taught that the real enemies are mutant creatures; two-headed, nuclear-infected savages who hide in ancient ruins like unused train tunnels. To me these just sound like tacky bedtime stories, but Serenity's biologists noted NORA as the scientific cause of the evolution of such beasts long ago. I've never seen them though, and until I do I can't confirm how hideous and violent they truly are. For all I know they'd be easier to live with than us. In my opinion, it was *human* nature, not mother nature, that prompted the destruction of what is now *Ad Infinitum*- or the old Earth.

NORA just finished the job and took the credit.

This in mind, I concentrate more on the chalk paintings and scarecrows than on any breathing bodies. I'm too tempted to end this earlier than planned; get it over with. So I adjust my aim for each moving dummy that passes by, using arrows because they are easy to make. Out there I'll never be short of sharp rocks and branches. Clean water and food maybe, but if I practise my aim I can eat birds and rabbits.

"Twelve, you're up. Hit the target," Zthora's voice echoes from the front of our dome-shaped training room. "Quickly now. You're running out of time."

I step up, draw my bow and take aim. The first arrow soars and stabs a swinging sack target in the upper thigh. I'd been aiming for the red cross painted on his chest. The room falls silent except for a mild chortle from Warden. I scowl but hold my tongue.

"Again!" she calls. "*Now*, Twelve!"

"*I'm trying*," I yell back. I snatch a second arrow from the stand beside me and curse myself for biting. "Goddammit!"

FFT is in place to help us determine friend from foe but Zthora leaves me painfully undecided. Half my will wants to aim for her head whilst the other wants to show Warden that I'm a survivor.

I try and fail once more, then snap the bow across my knee.

"That won't solve your problem," Corrina says. She's up next and is holding tight to her confident expression. "I think you're trying too hard. You need to exhale before you release."

Desperate to show her I'm capable I grab a knife instead, weighing the metal in my palm. Other options include swords, spears and spiked shields, none of which I'd wield well. I limber up to loosen my overalls. I shrug off my previous attempt.

"Damn arrows were bent. I'd like to see *you* do any better."

"Well I can't now, can I?" Corrina folds her arms. "Just throw, Twelve. I haven't got all day."

Aeon Infinitum: Run For Your Life

I flip the knife. Before I can throw I hear Warden's laughter. He stands nearby with his arm around Chastity. It's off-putting to say the least but Zthora gestures at me to begin despite the distraction. On my first throw the knife hits the target's edge and by my fifth there's straw on the floor. I celebrate when Corrina's secure expression begins to slacken.

"My number isn't Twelve for nothing," I tell her.

"Twelve *is* a great number," shouts Warden, "There will always be somebody tougher than you though. I'd remember that." He squeezes Chastity's shoulder. "Four, your time is better spent elsewhere."

When they've gone I wipe the sweat from my forehead. The swinging dummy slows to a stop and Corrina moves to the podium's edge to take over.

I grin. "Hey, the higher your rank, the harder your fall."

"I'll have to fall on you then," she says.

With Corrina's attention on the target and Chastity stood with the warden, I explore some solo exercises that have been constructed by Exigency's builders, designed to broaden my survival skills. There, I won't be disturbed or ridiculed.

First on my list is the assault course. Before I'm on my knees to navigate through a tunnel I clang my head and scrape my elbows. I'll need to tuck my limbs in next time. Although bloody and sore already, I continue because I'd be forced to in the wilderness but it isn't long before I'm forced to a halt to swallow a mouthful of vomit. Unexpected claustrophobia in the complete darkness of the tunnel unnerves me and an unknown acrid stench becomes overwhelming.

I force my legs to move after a few deep breaths. Sharp rocks slash at my skin as I pull my weight through a soup of earthy materials. Mud collects under my fingernails and splashes across my face.

It occurs to me as I pick at a strange splodge of brown on my arm that Serenity has used genuine materials. None of the leaves are cardboard. None of the dirt is painted (it may even be faeces, given the smell!). Zthora's team must have fought Czar's fear of contamination for weeks to create such a realistic training room. Perhaps they do want us to succeed after all?

Next in the sequence is a forest setting. I'm already covered in filth so it's easy to disappear but nevertheless, I take advantage of the paints provided. Camouflaged, I squat beneath a sheet of netting that's covered in green and brown leaves for a while and eventually see Chastity run by. Warden is screaming orders at her from the sidelines. Neither of them sees me.

Upper body strength will be equally important so I hoist myself up some frayed rope to test the strength in my limbs when they've moved on. After regaining my breath and admitting I'm not as fit as I should be, I find a platform to sit on and take a break. It's then that I notice how light and flexible Chastity actually is.

Manoeuvring at alarming heights doesn't seem to phase her, nor does underwater swimming. Heights and I have never agreed and I can swim, but not well. From the top of her own rope she plunges into a small swimming pool head first and glides through the water with complete confidence in every stroke. Each length takes mere seconds and I wonder how and where she learned to swim.

Titan's one and only public pool has been closed for the past twelve years. Apparently, a banished inmate polluted the water system in that sector and Czar had never bothered to waste resources on its sanitisation. Warden surely has access to Czar's private leisure centre hidden somewhere in this tomb. Precious Chastity could have easily taken advantage.

When I jump down to study her more, Corrina puts her hand on my shoulder.

"We can still save her. I know you think friendship is dangerous but she's just a kid."

"Concentrate on your own training. Can't you see Warden has her under his wing now? He's been enhancing her training. It's obvious he wants her to run, Corrina. He even taught her to swim. You won't be able to evade him."

"Don't you want to at least *try*?"

"Despite what you might think of me, my lack of interference is for her own good." I shake my shoulder free of her grip. "I suggest you leave me alone before Warden intervenes."

"There's nothing else he can do to me." Corrina folds her arms. "My death warrant has already been signed."

To avoid upsetting the kid, I gesture at Corrina to move away from the water.

"Wanna bet? Look, false hope won't help her. The more you encourage such nonsense, the less likely she'll be to survive this because she'll stop trying to prepare. Though I can't say death would be so terrible."

"*Death* is for her own good? You *can't* be serious."

Warden turns his head in time to catch me rolling my eyes. His own narrow as he keeps a close watch on our disagreement. I try to appear less conspicuous by turning to face him.

"How can you be this selfish? She's fourteen years old, Eden."

"So now I'm *Eden* and not Twelve? When you want something you soften. Are you through punishing me for refusing your friendship at the breakfast table? Don't take it personally. None of us can afford to get too close, Corrina. It'll only make what comes next more difficult. Listen to yourself. You want to sneak her away from the other Venturers and hope nobody finds where you stashed her. What happens when the running begins? When she's out of food and clean water? When everyone she's ever known has left this place and she's all alone, she'll have nothing but hatred for you."

"Better than running for Czar's so-called sanctuary and risking the wasteland."

"The Harmony Grid filters the weak. Chastity isn't strong enough to survive, though I'll admit she's surprised me so far. She needs to stay with us and train so she has something near a chance at survival. A fast, painless death *is* kinder but unfortunately a luxury. Stow her in here and she'll die alone when we abandon Titan. Stow her up top and she's a meal. The ending of this book is the same, Corrina, but *we* can decide the storyline. If she finishes her training and runs with us as planned, at least she can write the final chapter on her own."

"You witnessed her sessions just then," she reasons. "Fast swimmer. Excellent climber. She'll survive, I *know* she will. If she runs with us, what's to say she won't make it?"

I lower my voice. "Then let her find out. Remember, swimming and climbing are talents Czar *doesn't* need. We can't predict the future. Even if she does make it do you think Warden won't pay Czar off to banish her anyway? You heard the briefing; they'll guard the perimeter. In other words if they don't want you to live, you won't. If the mutants don't kill her, how long do you think it'll be before one of our own takes the shot?"

Corrina's bottom lip begins to quiver. Suddenly it dawns on her that I'm right and there's no way to save her.

"You're considering killing Chastity yourself, aren't you? Out there during the run. How can you be so cruel?"

Before her first tear falls I tell her I wouldn't make a move without good reason. When I glance at Warden his eyes are wide and overly interested, like he can already taste the bloodshed. I *hate* myself for being the reason he's smiling.

"I'm sorry, Corrina. If she's injured or bitten, I'll do for her what I hope you'd do for me. If she turns up at the gate with an infected wound, they may not be so kind."

"You're evil for even thinking it, Eden."

Warden sets off walking in our direction. Through gritted teeth I hiss back at her. I'm not evil. I'm logical.

"What you see is determination. Czar wants us to scout the so-called *safe sanctuary*. Nothing about this task is going to be safe or easy, Corrina. It's better to let luck decide Chastity's fate because, despite your efforts, you can't save everyone."

"So you'd kill an innocent kid and spare her what, a *future*?"

"A hideous death." I spit. "Czar brainwashed everyone to encourage this process. The people of Titan are pleased because they think he's helping to re-populate the planet. They see moving on as a step forward when actually he's doing the exact opposite *just* to save his own skin. The Harmony Grid sparks excitement for a new life but it just filters those Czar can't use. Chastity is one of them. As are we, really. End of story."

Warden calls, "Twelve, this is called the training room for a reason. Don't make me come over there."

I frown and lean forward. "Don't do anything stupid, *please*."

She'll ignore my words of advice. I sense it. We should both forget the kid's ties to the warden and concentrate on ourselves; hide from the likelihood that we'll meet a horrific fate or cover our ears and hum a pleasant tune until it's time. Too long have I been abandoned in a freezing cell to rot, been beaten and starved or eaten alive by rats. Now I can taste freedom, however temporary it is likely to be. I believe we all deserve a chance to experience it. By 'saving' Chastity, Corrina takes away that opportunity but I can do nothing more about it.

The warden orders us to wash and return to our cells a short time later. I scrub the filth from my body until my skin is raw, wearing the pain like my pride. I wrap my knees and elbows in soft bandage strips to pad today's wounds and clean the others of grit, then pull on a fresh pair of navy pants and an inmate issue shirt, complete with my number. Soon another unlucky inmate will inherit it and I feel as sorry for them as I did for myself on day one.

My only distraction is an old hardback book which I read for ten minutes until footsteps approach my cell. It's Warden. I can tell by his over-confident stride and the chink of the metal chains that decorate his black leather boots.

He hammers on the door before letting himself in and a young woman follows close behind. She is clutching a scroll and pencil to her chest.

Warden gestures at my visitor. "You have ten minutes. Be nice."

I tuck the book beneath my pillow. "I'm always nice."

Without a word more (but with a raised brow) he leaves us alone to talk.

I shake the woman's outstretched hand. "I don't get many visitors."

"I'm from Wardrobe. Unfortunate circumstances perhaps, but I'm pleased to meet you. Warden tells me you're dangerous and I shouldn't turn my back to you. Should I worry or are we good?"

I fold my arms and lean against the bunk. "Unless you signed my death warrant, Kid, I'd say we're good. What's a Wardrobe worker doing on death row anyway?"

The woman glances down at her things. "I brought my designs. We've created an outfit for your journey we think you'll like. Veil and I worked hard to get this approved by Needle and Thread. They think, with extra effort, that they can pull it off."

"*Veil?* Is that his nickname or something?"

She shakes her head, loosening the band holding back her brunette curls and then hands me her parchment. Her eyes are bold and speckled green. Her posture is gentle and nervous. Although she's wary of me, I read in her an eagerness to trust me and be, herself, trusted.

"He was a Venturer before he became a mentor for Wardrobe. He's been outside. I value his opinion. You should too."

I cross my fingers and gesture at the parchment. "Sounds like you're on my side then. Are there others in Wardrobe?"

"Some for the other inmates. Do you like this design or shall I have Veil pull it from the production line?"

I'll be a tree with brown fabric across my chest, green leaf-covered gloves, moss-coated boots and a helmet decorated with sprigs and flowers. Paint my face and I'll blend perfectly with the earth.

"At least I'll be invisible. Please thank your mentor for me."

"I will. We'll meet daily until the run. Veil wants to add more real flowers to mask your scent and throw off animals. Inside are pockets to hide food and weapons. Before I fill your pockets we'll have to check your allergies. Needle and Thread hate working with natural materials because they never agree with their stitching but I think we've convinced them to make an exception. After all, Titan's future might depend on your survival."

"No pressure then." I roll up the paper and hand it back, hoping for a change of topic. "What made you go for camouflage?"

"We incorporated a few new ideas into an old drawing that's all. It's been a long time coming, this Harmony Grid. Making the best of a poor situation is a talent of mine," she says. "Is there anything you want me to add? We have a few days left before production begins properly."

"How about some hidden compartments in my boots or my helmet. If I drop my bag I'm going to need a backup stash. Oh, and a harness for tree climbing? Shelter might be difficult so I need to be sure I can sleep anywhere securely. Heights and I don't agree but if it's the only safe place, it'll become a permanent one I'd imagine."

"A belt, extra pockets and a waterproof jacket are the best I can do."

"Sold."

She moves toward the door, taking backward steps as not to lose sight of me. "I should get back now. See you tomorrow, same time."

"Wait, I didn't catch your name."

"My name is Elvandra but you can call me Rae," she says. Rae extends her hand again and I accept willingly. "And you're Eden, right? It was nice meeting you."

The warden returns to take her back to Wardrobe and says nothing in the process. Once I'm alone, I lay on my bunk staring at the ceiling, imagining how easy this could be with Wardrobe's genius design. Soon it will be a hideous, distant memory, not only for me but for the community.

One thing I know for sure is that the lingering

monsters of *Ad Infinitum* are heading our way, if they're not plotting already. When the banished arrive too, using NORA's destruction to their advantage and declaring an inevitable war, Titan will finally fall.

I only hope we make it back in time.

6

Eden Maas

Although unannounced, the next time I see Warden he's alone and pale; almost sickly. I'm surprised when he knocks on the sliding metal panel before slipping inside my cell. I don't think he has knocked once in his life.

It takes a couple of minutes before he remembers why he's here and until he does we glare at one another in a thick, choking silence. Without permission, he sits beside me at the end of my bunk and turns the book I've been reading over in his hands. Then his mouth upturns as he flicks through the pages.

"It's beautiful, isn't it?" he asks, followed by a quote. "*Hope nevermore to look upon the heavens; I come to lead you to the other shore, to the eternal shades in heat and frost. And thou, that yonder standest, living soul, withdraw thee from these people, who are dead.*"

"Dante's Inferno," I tell him as he looks up with raised brows. "Classic and fitting given our circumstances. A few months ago I expected to meet my maker at the noose with a burdened heart and now I expect to meet a painful judgement day out in the wilderness. I'll be no more alive than the people of Titan though. If we Venturers fall, Titan falls with us. Your purpose in my life is to lead me to my death, not a safer shore."

Warden nods solemnly and sighs. "We are indeed in a *forest dark*." He slams the cover shut and throws the book down. "The straightforward pathway has been lost and our trust with it."

Startled by his quotation of Dante I retrieve the book and cradle it. I adored Dante way before my incarceration. The words are beautiful and constantly relevant to my life. Warden's perception of the words are quite dissimilar though, but he's not here to analyse poetry with me.

"A lack of trust between friends is no fault of mine," I tell him. "I'm in here for an assassination attempt, Warden. Why are *you* here?"

Warden frowns. "I'm in for the betrayal of your trust." He gestures at the book. "Our library is filled with treasures like that and I find it to be the one place free from my demons. I suggest you visit before the run. I'll authorise an escort if you're interested."

Warden closes his eyes and tilts his head low. He's trying to piece together another line from my precious book.

"*All those who perish in the wrath of God here meet together out of every land; and ready are they to pass o'er the river, because celestial Justice spurs them on, so that their fear is turned into desire.*'"

"Titan's demons are man-made, as are yours," I remind him, "though I suppose you could say the people living here *did* meet the wrath of God when Czar took the place of his wretched father. Warden, you didn't come here to analyse Dante, nor to talk about the past. To what do I *really* owe the pleasure?"

I replace my book on the only shelf in my cell and lean against the door with folded arms, temporarily blocking his exit.

"I'm here to visit."

"Rubbish. You either came to say goodbye and clear your conscience or ask something of me. Your visits are never selfless."

"You know me well," he says, forcing a weak smile. "I came to wish you luck on your journey, *all* of you."

Several minutes pass in silence until Warden's eyes find the book, probably because it's the only thing in the room that isn't grey or chained to the floor.

"Humans did one thing right," he says.

"Finally something we agree on. If you're going to stare, you should just take it; I can't carry the weight of Dante in my pack," I tap my skull. "I'll have the words with me anyway."

As I offer it out, Warden shakes his head and gestures that I put it back. "You keep it and think about what I said."

"You haven't said much though, have you?"

"Are you going to make me beg?" he asks.

"I don't need Dante to remind me how to be human, Warden. I'm a killer, not a murderer. I know why you're here so save your breath. You're asking me to save Chastity but I can't, not when I can barely protect myself. If you're in love then *you* save her. A prison warden has to have some sway on the governor."

"There's no difference between being a killer and a murderer, Eden," he mutters through barred teeth.

"Death is death. You just need to try harder in training. You're slacking. They are going to need a leader out there and you're capable but too stubborn."

"Is that why I'm being banished? To protect your lover?" I shake my head in disbelief. "Death is unfortunate but the circumstances make all the difference, Warden. Once you understood that and agreed Czar's methods were ridiculous. You even offered to help me rid Titan of his influence, remember? Back *then* you weren't so naïve and selfish. You talk as though you give a damn if I live. What changed? Your feelings toward the kid, right?"

Warden avoids eye contact. "My nerve, I think. You didn't deserve what I did to you, Eden and neither does Chastity. So I'm asking you to help her because you're strong. I've seen your resilience and bravery these past few months, and I've been cruel. Czar couldn't know you and I were lovers. I can't imagine what might have happened if-"

This is unbelievable. "Don't pretend to be on my side when you're here to beg for Chastity's life, not for the forgiveness you can never earn. *You* put me in here because you claimed it would 'save my life' and instead all you've done is ridicule and abuse me by dangling that stupid kid in my face, so why *should* I save her life or even try? You used my imprisonment as an excuse to separate *your* innocence from *my* guilt. But you're not innocent, are you? The whole plan was your idea! I'm sorry but Chastity is going to die, Warden. Get used to it."

His face reddens. He cracks his knuckles. "I shouldn't have to ask but I am. I thought there might still be an ounce of empathy left in that heart. The Eden I knew would've put a child's life before her own, but I guess nobody would place blame if you decided to abandon this entire quest and opt for death instead. If you're so sure Chastity will die I guess you've doomed yourself too. Shall I file the paperwork?"

I spit at his feet. "Do your worst. I'm practically a child myself."

Warden flinches as hurried footsteps pass the cell and I find myself smirking.

"Sounds like they're missing you, Warden. Shall I call them in here?"

"I'm supposed to be in a meeting and no," he grumbles. "We're not done here."

"Oh, we are. Thanks for the offer to hang but I'll take my chances at freedom," I tell him. "Nice to see you're considerate of others though."

Warden rolls his eyes and stands abruptly. "I know you hate me. Think I'm a monster if you must but I'm not here to gloat. I only came to ask that you protect her. She's a *child*, Eden."

To prevent laughter I bite my fist and squeeze my eyes closed. "Why recommend her for banishment if you love her so much, or *me* for that matter? We have history, more so than you and Chastity. You're using me to protect my replacement. How do you think that makes me feel?"

Warden unbuttons the collar on his shirt and paces the cell, hands on hips. He's nervous. Too nervous.

"If you can't answer me-"

"I can't, Eden, I just can't, all right? I have my reasons and they're for your own good. Can't you just trust me? You both need to leave Titan and survive out there."

"Pfft. I'm not convinced you care what happens to Chastity; you just want to make sure *one* of us comes back so Titan doesn't eat itself alive down here. Did Czar send you to sweet talk me?"

"Is your heart so hard?" he asks. "Prison has changed you; made you selfish."

"*You* did that. Ever since you intervened in my sentence all you've done is make my life hell. You were my co-conspirator and you wiped your hands of me to avoid the same fate. *I've* toughened up and you should too. I can survive this on my own. Why would I let you hang me now when I'm *so* close to getting out of here? Best of all I'll be far far *far* away from *you*. Wardrobe's design can guarantee me that."

Warden's eyes follow me around the cell. His fists are clenched; it's taking all he's got not to strike me.

"Wardrobe won't save the others though," he replies. "I don't think you could leave behind those who helped you. Elvandra Rae is an innocent peasant in comparison, with no stamina or determination."

"What's your point?"

"Do you want to be tied to liabilities? Of course not," Warden says, "You're a lone wolf. Elvandra is hoping you'll come back to save her and Donar, Eden. If you run and never come back, you're signing her death warrant."

"What do *you* care? You're as much a killer as I am. You hated Czar and you'd have left Titan behind too in my shoes. By returning here there's no guarantee any of them will live anyway. They still have to run for their lives."

Warden gets to his feet and extends a hand. "The choice is yours in the end but I wanted you to know that I *am* sorry for everything, Eden, and despite your efforts to isolate yourself there are others who care and rely on you." Warden opens the cell door. I stand with my back against the wall. "Think about it."

"I heard you the first time. Will that be all, Warden?"

"Suit yourself. I care for Chastity as I once cared for you, Eden. I see it in your face how close you are to forgiveness and sacrifice. If you can, swallow your bitterness. Wouldn't want to die with regrets now, would you?"

"I don't plan on dying at all."

I grab the book from my shelf as he turns to leave and thrust it into his chest. I'm so tired of playing games; he needs to know how insignificant he's made me feel since my sentence and Dante, I'm sure, can help me achieve that.

"'*Still not a tear I shed, nor answer made all of that day, nor yet the night thereafter, until another sun rose on the world'*," I quote. "The sun *will* rise again, Warden, on a beautiful, *free* world for the human race."

He steps into the corridor, smiling. "A future I look forward to, then."

7

Ginny Bede

After breakfast I meet Rachana as I'm heading to my dorm. This entire sector is dimly lit. Evenly mounted oil lamps line the labyrinth of passages which are all arched. It's eerie during the dark months and impossible to see past the lamp ahead.

An hour ago I filed Rachana's transfer papers from Rehab to Expediency. She's young and healthy so I thought she'd be happier there. She's standing outside my dorm shaking those papers in fury so I guess I was wrong, and it's too late to skulk out of sight now.

"Why not Serenity, Ginny?" she asks. A scowl sets upon her brow. "In your way, *am I*?"

"If I thought Serenity would take you then that's where you'd be. Don't you trust my judgement?"

"Your report didn't exactly boost my ego. I thought we were friends."

I sigh and wring my palms together. "I want you to benefit from your faction so I recommended Expediency. Either that or prostitution but we've already established you're not up for that. Look, Serenity plan and organise and I just don't think you'd do well here. You'll get bored. You're intelligent but as you're young I want to put all this energy and enthusiasm into a physical job."

Rachana storms off down the corridor sending echoes of rustling and footsteps in both directions. Soon I'm jogging to keep pace so I don't lose sight of her.

"I *am* your friend."

"I'll bet that's what you tell all the orphans."

"If you'd let me explain-"

Rachana stops and folds her arms. "I'm listening."

Age must be taking its toll. I have to lean forward and take a second to catch my breath before I can offer any defence.

"Expediency staff learn all kinds of skills and your value as a citizen will increase. Without you there's no warning system or understanding of the entry methods and timing of the banished, who crawl in through abandoned caves, create diversions, steal food, water, disable locking mechanisms and cause chaos. Expediency is our *only* protection against their mayhem."

"This isn't fair, Ginny. I'm better than this!"

I pull Rachana aside as an armed guard passes us on routine patrol. Czar will re-assess her value in Expediency against how likely she is to begin an uprising or start a riot if she's too outspoken. An opinion can get you killed here.

"For your own good, take the job and keep your voice down, kid. Venturers disappear for six months and race against time to avoid the darkness. You said yourself that I'd put you off the job so why argue? Humans experimented with nuclear technology and biological warfare before NORA struck. Imagine what the damage leaked; *created*. They risk their lives to gather what is likely to be useless information and then die early. The other alternative is a job like mine where you'll be bored all day, every day. I thought you'd appreciate something in the middle."

"Can you at least pull some strings and get me assigned to the watchtower?" she asks, her brow raised.

"Deal." Anything to keep her quiet. "Rachana, I told you I've never made a mistake before and I'm not about to start so will you just take the job?"

A lock of orange falls loosely across her almond-shaped face and I brush it back. She softens. "Fine, whatever. I *guess* I trust you."

"Gee, thanks. On the bright side, you won't be reading useless research data and hating my guts for a living."

"Research data is *never* useless, only interpreted incorrectly. A little like you're doing with me now." She heads off down the corridor but halts beneath the next lamp. Her hair glows like fire beneath it. "I'd better find Warden. He's in charge of the tower. We have to co-sign the paperwork. I'll see you later."

On that note, she disappears. I linger, glaring after her and wondering if I've made the right choice. Have I interpreted her mind incorrectly? No way. I couldn't live with myself if anything happened to her. Expediency it is, and Expediency it shall remain.

"Ginny, where's your new recruit?"

My heart thumps against my rib cage. "Warden, you *scared* me. Rachana went to find you," I tell him. "She needs her paperwork signing off. I assigned her to Expediency. The council will be pleased. She's enthusiastic and eager to learn, unafraid of hard labour and young. Shall I go after her?" Silence falls between us until I gather the courage to question his presence. "Everything all right?"

"She's reading *Dante*."

Warden shuffles in his suit as though it's itching him. His brown eyes look like black pits in this light, illuminated only when an occasional tear travels the length of his nose. I slap a firm hand on his back. Poor Warden; forced to send the woman he loves into the wilderness but with good reason. Czar insisted she be hung months ago, but Warden couldn't go through with it. Instead, Czar suggested she take her chances outside and be put to work. Until now Warden's been unable to sign the release form so she's been rotting in prison in the meantime.

I miss Eden's presence in Rehab. She was a hard-working, loyal member of Serenity.

He hands me the book, saddened by the sight of its crusty cream pages and tattered cover. "Am I a coward?"

"Are you asking as a friend or as the prison warden?"

"A friend, Gin. *Always* a friend," he says.

"You're a coward but death *is* scary," I tell him "Assassinating the governor was a good idea at the time but it was reckless too. Had Eden not been so desperate and waited for your signal, the knife wouldn't have missed his heart. Things might be different."

"If only," he sighs, "but I had to explain it somehow!"

"If you both admitted your guilt, neither of you would be alive now. It's a fact that Eden acknowledges.

Give her time."

Warden rubs his face, tired of lying and scheming his way around our justice system.

"Eden and I would have been executed. She asked me to let Czar kill her but how could I? There *is* no time because it's true that Titan can no longer support its population. I take comfort in knowing she'll be free to explore the surface but I'm afraid she'll never come back. The rest of us are going to die down here, suffer sanction after sanction until Titan is no more, Gin. I'm pleased she and Chastity will be out of here soon. I don't trust our stability. What do I do? How am I supposed to react?"

"All relationships are a death sentence in Titan. It's my job to understand people and I think you did your best to save her life."

Warden slumps against the wall, barely missing the lamp above his head. "She hates me. I've treated her terribly."

"For her own good to throw off suspicion. I'd have done the same and so would she."

"I'm going to talk to Wardrobe and see if I can pull some strings. If I can increase the inmates' rations or wrangle some additional ammunition I'll feel better." Warden's hands begin to shake. "Got anything to calm the nerves?"

"Back at my place, maybe."

I'm about to invite him back but my nerves get the better of me. How will it look if Warden and I are caught drunk, sharing sob stories about his failed relationship surrounded by my stash of illegal substances? Our allegiance against Czar had never been made public for obvious reasons.

"Drinking away your sorrows won't erase your cowardice and if they catch us together for anything other than a business-related conversation, we'll be running alongside Eden. You can't help her if you're dead so I think you should go home."

His fists clench. "No, I was hoping we could talk more. I need your help, Gin. You *have* to talk to Eden in her Rehab session. She's refusing to protect Chastity."

I shake my head. "You can't force people to make friends and Eden worked here, Warden, so she knows how to cheat the system. How can you expect her to trust you or anyone else after everything she's been through? Took you long enough to trust *me*, remember?"

Warden's face reddens. "I'm not asking you to brainwash her-"

"I know what you're asking and the answer is still no. You should go home. It's getting late and in about an hour the guards will switch shifts."

"What difference does *that* make?" he asks. "It doesn't solve my problem!"

"Eden's running out of time to get her revenge, Warden. You ruined her life and in a few days, she'll be free of this place. If she can escape tonight she will and guess whose name is going to be at the top of her list?"

Warden scowls. His face turns pale. "I'll increase the security in Sector C. Just think about what I said, Gin and we'll talk more tomorrow, if I'm still alive."

8

Elvandra Rae

Six days later...

The due-to-be-banished inmates sit opposite Donar and me in Wardrobe's main hall. Neither side was prepared for a meeting at such short notice; most of us met with our allocated inmates days ago. My logic tells me there's something else going on.

The night staff, including the cleaning shift, have been asked to leave and in their place, Warden's own prison guards are at the exits to the hall. Our concerned expressions tell me we're all anxious to find out why we've been summoned here so late. Only an hour ago Donar and I were asleep in our dorm, dreaming of better days to come so I hadn't been given a chance to change from my nightclothes before we were roused and asked to attend. I'm underdressed and self-conscious but I imagine so is everyone else.

Although my stomach is churning with fear I take some comfort in Veil's unusual posture. Rather than the upright statue he usually portrays, today he's slumped forward like he's dozing. I'm pleased because these are signs that he's something other than an empty cavity when he taps his pencil and foot in unison. In the dead silence that has settled between the two groups, I begin to twitch. Torn between manners and patience, I slam down my hand on the bench to silence Veil's repetitive noise.

"We're not here to be driven insane, Veil," I tell him before I attempt to confiscate the pencil. "We're here for a reason."

"A reason none of us knows," Donar says.

He's been twirling a dirty fork between his fingers, flicking gravy in all directions, for the past ten minutes. Twice I have scowled at him to no avail. His greying hair is dishevelled and silvery in the dim candlelight and he glares at Veil, equally as irritated by the tapping but less aware of the splashes of old food than he should be. Veil peels my palm off his pencil and snaps the lead in two, his eyes never leaving mine.

Eden raises a brow and leans back in her seat, arms folded. She's probably disappointed he hasn't grabbed my fingers instead.

"This whole thing is a waste of time," she grumbles, "and another night's sleep wasted."

"Ignore her she's grumpy," Corrina says. She and Eden glare at one another, eyes unblinking. "Eden's slept with one lid open for the past five months anyway."

"*Somebody* organised this," says Juliette. "It's clear from the lack of information that we have to figure out who ourselves." My mouth must twist as I'm pondering possibilities because she says, "I'm more worried about the *why*, aren't you Elvandra?"

When I don't reply, Eden leans forward. "Got any ideas, Rae?"

"Hey, don't look at me. I thought Warden arranged it for you guys. Those are his guards out there. The Harmony Grid has an imminent effect on all of us here, so it'd be wise to discuss our options and how our jobs here intertwine. We need to come up with a sane plan to survive Czar's actions. Personally, I think Warden has given us all a break and a chance to speak freely. Any other suggestions?"

Eden grins. "If Warden set this up then, believe me, it's for personal gain only. *I'd* say he's trying to force us together so we'll agree to protect his prized possession." Eden glances at the young blonde girl sat a few seats down, but when neither she nor I reply, Eden laughs. "This is just *golden*. None of you Wardrobe folk has any idea what I'm talking about." She glances at Corrina who rolls her eyes. "Did *you* have anything to do with this?"

"Yeah 'cos I'm *all* about helping you, Eden. Sorry but I'm not guilty. Bigger fish to fry at the moment; I took your advice. Don't seem so surprised."

There's an inmate present that none of us has met before but he mustn't know why we're here either. The kid hasn't moved or made a sound yet. His name is Amani and he's a dark haired, slender boy of about seventeen years. I'm assuming from his entwined fingers that he'd rather not share a bench with the dangerous strangers, so he sits alone on the next one in the row of ten. Perhaps he knows more than he's letting on but I also assume that (as all three inmates are now aware of Eden's crime) like most Titan citizens he's probably mortified that he's even in the same room as her.

I don't know much about the event that landed her on death row and I dare not ask for the history.

"Amani, do you want to sit on our bench?" He looks up but doesn't reply. "Being the only male inmate in this month's banishments means you probably don't know the others yet. They separate you in training, right?"

Eden groans. "That's how it needs to stay."

"Don't be rude," Juliette says. "Imagine being the only female. How might you feel?"

In the candlelight, Eden's wide eyes are luminous with fury. It sends shudders of fear down my spine.

"*Relieved.* Amani seems an awful lot quieter than this rabble," she replies. "Maybe then I'd get some sleep."

"Warden probably wants Wardrobe to organise more fittings or something," Donar suggests with a shrug.

Eden shakes her head. "Whether your designs fit will be the least of our worries. All I've been able to think about is being eaten alive or starved. Of course, I could drown or be ripped apart. How about mutated? Maybe poisoned! And all before you lot know whether you're staying or going. We know our plan of action is to run for our lives. What's yours?" When none of us replies, Eden says, "So obviously this meeting wasn't arranged to help our side. It has something to do with Wardrobe."

"Perhaps we're here to say goodbye to one another?"

The attention of our table is drawn toward Amani. His voice is light and delicate; the opposite of how I'd imagined he'd sound. Although his frame is small and his face young, he's muscular and comfortable in his skin.

"We're not that close," Eden says. "Why not just go

back to your cell, Amani? This doesn't concern you."

"Why not?"

I'm about to ask what Eden means when she says, "If the plan is to run together, Amani is probably your best hope. That's the impression I got from his FFT anyway."

"You didn't witness my FFT," he replies, confused.

Eden gestures at his hands. "I didn't need to."

Amani hides the grazes across his knuckles but doesn't reply. Perhaps she's right about him. None of the Wardrobe workers witness how their allocated inmate has been progressing in their physical sessions, nor in their rehabilitation.

"Need I go on?"

Eden is pleased with herself now but beneath the intimidating demeanour, she's a sweet woman with a deeply rooted fear of death. To prove otherwise she begins to pace the length of the bench, moving toward Amani's seat. If she's good at anything, I've learned, it's getting under the skin of her enemies.

"Don't be ashamed, Amani. You'll be the last of us to die."

Veil glares at her from beneath his robes. "Eden, *sit down*."

"Are you going to make me?" She re-focuses her attention on the candidate most likely to bite. "You've been quiet too, Veil. Take off that hood. I've heard rumours about what it's hiding."

Eden clenches her fists and slams them both down in front of her target, causing the others to jump. Veil never flinches.

"Eden, I wouldn't poke the bear."

She ignores me.

"Could be this hooded maniac's fault," she says.

Veil's voice is flat when he replies, "You are under the impression that I have something to add."

"You've been too evasive to suggest anything else, Veil. You're not one of them, you're one of *us*. You were an inmate so I know you don't want to be friends with anyone here. You're a killer. Somebody- most likely Warden- arranged this meeting for a reason. I think that reason is *you*."

"I am not an inmate now, nor am I a maniac," he replies, "and I am loyal to no-one. I am here for the same reason as you, which it would seem is currently a mystery."

Eden growls and decides to taunt the others instead, realising she'll get little more from Veil. Donar flinches when his mentor, Juliette, reaches out and snatches her arm.

"Sit down, Eden. Think about how your behaviour affects your colleagues."

"*Colleagues*? I don't even like half of you. We're all *inmates*. Anti-social, disruptive, uncommunicative criminals. I'll warn you against expecting anything else. Now I'm going back to my cell; there's no hope here."

"If he's given us this opportunity, Warden disagrees," Juliette argues.

"This isn't going to be a bonding exercise, Juliette. We're all too far gone to reintegrate into the Titan community now. Chastity is fourteen and has never, *ever* seen daylight. If she goes outside in the light months, she'll no doubt be blinded. Corrina got sentenced for disagreeing with Czar's methods of citizen control.

Translated, that means murder. If she goes outside, Czar will *never* let her return. I'm here because I tried to terminate a disease. Do you think Czar is going to encourage four criminals to make friends with one another, then with a bunch of helpless Wardrobe staff and with this inhumane *alien*?"

Veil's fingers twitch but he refrains from retaliating.

"Ah forget it. None of you wants to accept what's really about to happen here."

Donar rubs his eyes. "Convince us quicker because I'm tired."

"Warden wants us to be afraid. Think about it. Of the people present Warden's only trusting connection is with Veil. Nobody else has wasteland experience. Am I right, Veil? Are you here to show us how Czar disposes of nuisance peasants?" says Eden.

Six days since the Harmony briefings and already Czar has his people's sanity on the brink of extinction. Uncomfortable, I shuffle out from the bench and stretch my legs.

"I don't think Veil knows anything, Eden, but perhaps *I* do." The room's attention shifts from Veil to me. "Warden and I had a conversation yesterday." I inhale and try not to look anyone in the eye as I move between the two benches. "I believe both sides of this group can make it across the Harmony Grid. If humans within Titan deem their duty is re-population and world domination then who am *I* to question Czar's orders? Sounds like the only way to initiate our future. It's a good thing, surely?"

"You told Warden this?" Eden asks, frowning.

"In not so many words. I told him that humans are

pack animals. If the citizens are willing to protect one another then perhaps we might show Czar that collectively we're not so expendable."

Eden shakes her head. "Elvandra, don't be naïve. Czar's reasons for activating the Harmony Grid have nothing to do with any of those things. It's personal gain and survival of the fittest."

I continue, ignoring her negativity. "Wardrobe is frightened the venturers won't return to save Titan and that Czar will send us all out there anyway, blind to the landscape." Before Eden can protest I growl at her and say, "Yes, Eden, I told him that too!"

"*Why* would you tell that man anything so personal?"

"Because we won't make it on our own. None of us has any combat experience. I know prison can't have convinced its residents to love this community but we need friends if survival is an option. We need one another. I think he listened and gave us chance to talk this through in private. He's doing us a favour."

"Half of Wardrobe isn't even here," Donar says. "I want to believe you, though. I'm scared too."

"Those of us Warden has a connection with are," I reply. "Eden is Warden's biggest problem and I can see why. He's been overseeing Chastity's training and Eden is the way to keep Chastity safe. Donar and I are the designers for you both and our mentors are Veil and Juliette. He's given our team an opportunity."

"What about us?" Corrina asks, "Amani and I don't fit in your theory."

"Maybe you're here to infuriate me," Eden snipes, then she rolls her eyes. "Elvandra's on to something, *maybe*. Warden saw Corrina and me together in training the other day."

"That leaves Amani," says Donar, "and doesn't explain why the other designers and mentors aren't here."

"The inmates are present to hear our plea for help and only our team was selected because it was me who raised the issue. At the end of the day, it won't matter why."

Eden sniggers. "Elvandra, if you know Warden like *I* know Warden it would. He's unpredictable. Separating the teams to incite fear is more his style, not to assist our survival."

"He's given us chance to ensure nobody is left behind to die," I reason. "Can't you see that?"

"Nobody is leaving anybody behind so you needn't worry," Corrina says. "Only cowards and betrayers walk away from opportunities like this. Both sides have something the other needs so we'll stick together."

"Oh, you are all so *weak*!" Eden inhales and slumps back on the bench, tapping the wooden leg with her boot. "Friendships sound great but what happens when your *friend* is being attacked and you're torn between saving their life and giving your own, or saving your own and letting their terrible luck finish them off? Can anyone here *honestly* say they'd choose the former? Sorry, Elvandra, but I can't agree with you. Friendships will get you all killed."

"I'm not so sure," Corrina interjects, "You and *I* aren't friends and I could kill you now without batting an eyelid."

Eden rolls up her sleeves and makes haste toward

Corrina. Veil grabs hold of her shirt before she can swing.

"I'd like to see you try."

"Stop it! This is what Czar *wants*. Imagine if we all arrive together," I tell Eden. "Czar can't turn us *all* away."

She picks at her nails, defeated. "He could."

Corrina rolls her eyes. "Eden, let's just do our job."

"It's not a job, it's a death sentence!"

"You will all be dead before you reach Titan's boundary, so I suggest you go back to your dorms," says Veil.

The group silences in awe and turns to him. His hands creep from beneath his robes and they are shaking, most likely in anger. The group gasps in unison when he lowers his hood. Hidden beneath that dark material are spider webs of scars, pockmarks, deep gouges in the shape of a jawline over which the skin has healed but become discoloured. He also has some strange looking tattoos that aren't in English nor any other language I can identify. I notice his left eye is blind and white except for the bulging red vein across the eyelid. His eyebrow splits in two on that side and his nose is badly misshapen.

I already knew of Veil's pain but have never seen his face up close before.

"What *happened* to you?" Chastity asks, unable to tear her eyes from his alarming appearance. "You're so-"

Veil's mouth presses into a thin line and his eyes narrow. The piercing green on his right side is predominant upon the pale canvas of his face. Veil scans the inmates, then settles on Chastity.

"Are you afraid?" he asks.

Her palms begin to sweat and she wipes them on her trouser legs, unable to meet Veil's gaze.

"So was I. Terrified, in fact. I have nothing to add to your conversation as it seems you have made the decision to befriend one another. Eden is right. It *is* unwise. I can only share my own experiences. Perhaps Warden knew you would come to this decision. Perhaps my presence is intended to dissuade you, as Eden suggested earlier, or persuade you. I am not Warden so I cannot speculate further." After a short pause, Veil begins. "When they banished me, they herded us into a bay with high metal walls and a domed ceiling like cattle to the slaughter. Our whimpers echoed back, filling the room with almost twice its capacity of souls. I broke down in tears."

"How many of you were there?" Donar asks.

"Banishment groups were greater then. Perhaps twenty. Unable to control myself, I gripped the hand of a young man beside me whose face I will never forget. He had light brown hair and hazel eyes with long lashes and a pleasant, comforting smile. Although he no doubt knew the procedure was somehow off, he held me casually and without fear.

"We thought our roles through Rehab would be based on the surface but within the boundaries of the ark, counselling hard working, fearful farmers. We were Expediency staff on temporary assignment as they could not spare any of Serenity at the time. Doors slammed behind us, closing off all entrances to Titan's main facilities. Every candle flickered and an unusual alarm blasted so loud that if I close my eyes and concentrate, I can still hear it.

"Ahead of us we heard grinding like stone cogs crashing against one another. The exit barriers began to rise, however where we expected to see bright sunlight there were stars and a blast of bitterly cold air, carrying flakes of snow inward. None of us was equipped for winter; they had released us early with few supplies. My shoes were tattered and unsuitable and my water bottle only half full. Czar had lied to us. The ark needed volunteer banishments. Decisions were made for us and nature would do the rest."

"I thought you were in prison?"

"For a short while. I participated in a rally against cuts to rations and was arrested for public order offences. I agreed to work off my sentence on the surface.

"We were shoved forward. A guard with a long electrical rod struck me across the shoulders and I sank, spasms of pain causing my body to thrash uncontrollably. Panic set in. Bodies were scrambling to the back, knocking into one another. I squinted through the darkness whilst being dragged against the crowd. That is when I saw them for the first time; the figures. They paced like starved lions, their eyes sparkled in the little light our compound cast across the wasteland. At first, I thought the gates held beacons; maybe there were other workers guiding us forward with torches. Maybe they marked a perimeter.

"The man I held yanked me aside before I registered that those flames were in fact warnings to whomever or whatever lurked, as a deterrent. He moved with confidence, separating from the gathering of citizens.

Before I could catch my breath we set off running; bolted away from the others and fled the scene. Screams pierced the silence. I followed my friend for miles unquestioningly, escaping unharmed. Together we hid in the trees, high enough to be free from danger but low enough to jump without breaking a bone. He told me to sleep and I must have."

Veil covers his mouth. His hand is shaking violently now. Whatever he's about to tell us he must be re-living.

"When I opened my eyes I saw my friend hung upside down with his legs tangled in the branches. His face had been mauled by cannibals and they paced at the bottom, waiting for dessert."

Veil pauses to take a breath. He replaces the hood as if to protect himself from the memory, swallows hard, and then continues his tale. None of us dares speak.

"I began to climb higher to evade the same fate but my foot slipped and sent me tumbling, pulling branches and leaves down on top of us both. I landed cushioned on the body but as I regained my balance and glanced up, there was the maimed face of our enemy. It had an unusual transparency as though a thousand fireflies swarmed its belly.

"I was bleeding and had broken my ankle but I hardly noticed. From the branches there were lacerations to my eyelid and brow, blinding me. I have suffered limited sight since. It took several minutes to feel the discomfort of my broken nose. Even with my vision blurred I knew I would be haunted by this creature forever. I took off running in the opposite direction and never looked back.

"Although exhausted and unable to continue from

the shooting pain in my foot, I managed to outrun it. I built a small, weak shelter with rocks and foliage, emerging from the moist hideout to hunt when the growling in my stomach threatened to give away my position."

Donar clears his throat. "Do you think that whatever killed your friend was once, uh, *human*?"

"It walked upright. Half the body was clothed but in rags, like remnants of an existence or identity to which it still clung. The other half was a tainted, possessed soul. I remember thinking I was being punished for my crimes by a demon."

"And was it, a, uh, a ghost?" Chastity asks.

"No. A creature evolved to survive the new landscape I think. All this time we believed the world to be dead from nuclear radiation, disease and global warming but I assure you it is quite the opposite. One day I awoke to a brighter morning. Not complete, but a definite sign of a sunrise somewhere. I gathered my few supplies and headed back to the ark, praying if they saw my injuries they might take pity."

"You were quarantined?" asks Eden.

Veil nods. "I had been bitten by so many strange animals, stung by various insects and fed on the flesh of infected meat that Czar feared I would plague the ark or spread disease. When they cleared me after several weeks of isolation, I was advised nobody my age had ever dared return after banishment. Those who had were shot on sight. Czar interviewed me himself and listened to my experiences but in honesty, I remember very little. Most of my first week I spent unconscious. He allowed me to stay having proven my bravery and willingness to 'report back with my findings', as though the entire ordeal was actually a mission I had survived. This is all I remember. My memory fades. I took basic accommodation and agreed to work as a mentor. Wardrobe fashioned my hood to cover my identity. Czar decided my injuries would frighten the citizens."

"Then what happened?" I ask.

"Life continued as though nothing happened."

Bewildered, the inmates (and surprisingly even Eden), are speechless. I unwind my fingers and exhale. I hadn't realised I'd been so tense through the anecdote and despite the terror in Veil's voice during his recollection, I feel relieved. I'm relieved he survived perhaps, or maybe because the tale is finally over.

"I know he died but he saved your life, Veil. Aren't you grateful for that short friendship?"

He shakes his head. "That mangled corpse has haunted my conscience ever since. He saved my life but I was unable to return the favour. I cannot help but think how direct he was upon our release. He must have known the beasts would attack the congregation instead of individual targets. I hope you are all smart enough to realise that whilst friendships may save you at first, you will all be alone eventually. Only then will your minds dig deep into those naturally evolved survival instincts."

"Veil, do you think you could do it again? I mean, survive on the wasteland that is."

Eden's jaw drops. I hold up my free hand to pause her argument, shaking my head. I know Veil better than most at this table. He'll be brutally honest with me. After a few moments of thought Veil nods, stands and makes haste for the door. Before leaving he turns and removes his robes completely, revealing a bare but completely tattooed chest.

"As you can see I have no room for new scars, but there will be no more cowering in darkened corners," he says.

Before any of us can question him, he is gone.

9

Eden Maas

The Harmony Grid map arrives at our final training session along with three of Czar's most qualified Venturers. Experienced and lightning fast, Aarya, Esmee and Xander enter the room with heads high, silencing Wardrobe and the other inmates with their overpowering confidence.

Their clothes are unusual and awkward; I can't imagine Wardrobe's logic behind mirrored chest panels and floral fabric because these Venturers are advertising every human weakness possible. Our lack of camouflage, clumsiness, egos and blatant need for attention. Outfits like those belong on Earth, not *Ad Infinitum,* though I'm sure an explanation is imminent.

Wardrobe are whispering and referring to sections of Aarya's uniform. Relief washes through my veins. Rae may be fragile since Czar's announcement- the way she moves and speaks delicately- but her knowledge in this field means everything to my survival. So long as she's smiling I'm satisfied and more importantly alive.

Zthora follows Czar's Venturers in and closes the door behind her. Xander begins preparations by removing the swimming pool's cover, laying out some weapons and bringing in Wardrobe's designs on a rolling cork board. Aarya assesses us; a permanent scowl on her face as though words are an inconvenience and we're all the ugliest beasts she's ever had to coach. Esmee appears to be their spokesperson and she's polite in comparison. Zthora introduces them.

"Aarya, Xander and Esmee are here to talk about your Harmony Grid routes, highlight the dangers and provide some life-saving advice. Pay attention. Warden will be by soon."

After her brief order she disappears without locking the door. We're in the presence of Czar's three most experienced assassins; she mustn't see the need for additional security.

Esmee outstretches a hand and introduces herself, offering a shake to anyone willing. I hesitate and accept but hold a firm face. Friendships are built on trust. For now, we can't rely on anyone Czar throws at us. I don't care if they're in uniform.

"Warden wanted this group to be together for your final FFT session. We're pretty excited to begin. The Harmony Grid has been explored several times but never this extensively so you'll be lucky to see the ruins and learn some history."

"Why are Wardrobe here for FFT?" asks Donar. "We were never given permission before."

Xander's growling voice booms across the training room from somewhere amongst the fake forest setting. Props are his main responsibility today.

"Warden is giving you a gift. Be grateful," he says.

Further questions are held until the end of their presentation which consists of some interesting acrobatics, demonstrating the flexibility of a Venturer and rough sketches of the mutants they've met since accepting the job in Exigency. As well as a physical and visual display of their own skills, Esmee insists we should each offer our own show of agility and determination, followed by advice to Wardrobe. I couldn't believe it before, but Rae was right. Warden is throwing them a life raft.

A hand is raised. "As fascinated by your backflips and irrelevant somersaults as I'm sure we *all* are, is there a purpose to this time wasting?" asks Corrina. She and I grin at one another. Finally, something we agree on. "I need survival advice, not circus antics and mediocre art."

Aarya raises her palm and moves swiftly. She strikes Corrina in the neck and once down, kicks her feet out from under her. She hits the ground with a thunk, bottom first, and groans. I hold my breath in anticipation as Corrina struggles to recover from the awkward fall.

"I didn't waste time there now, did I?"

I kneel by her side and lower my voice, then extend a hand. "Save your anger," I say.

Hesitant but with my aid Corrina stands and rubs her lower back. She limps aside. It looks like she's twisted her ankle and her ego is bruised but otherwise, she's unharmed.

Aarya returns to her silent stance by the training room door and averts her gaze.

I'm impressed. Amazing speed and a toned physique suggest continual practice and whilst her hair is loose and wild, accompanied by angry mud-brown eyes and thin lips, Aarya is still attractive and deadly. Drained of all emotion she's the perfect weapon against an unknown post-apocalyptic world. Brave, intelligent and hard-hearted. One day I hope to be just like her.

Esmee sighs. "Despite first impressions, we aren't gymnasts, artists or *barbarians*."

Aarya raises an eyebrow. "Nor as we push-overs."

"Each picture is a Venturer's creation from memory, not imagination," says Esmee. "Where there is a red cross, this marks a weakness. You need to know them all, just in case."

Xander reveals others, pinning them to the board and pointing at various aspects. Wings. Teeth. Claws. Fire. Fallen structures. So much death and destruction interpreted through their eyes. Understanding the situation, Chastity takes hold of Donar's hand and he yanks her into a warm embrace, muttering reassurances. She is utterly terrified and suddenly, so am I.

"I present a range of enemies," Xander says. He rolls up his already tight sleeves to reveal chunky, tanned arms, then scratches his shaven head. "Not just animals. Other banished inmates; people you replaced in prison. *Promotions*, Warden calls them. Each dance Esmee demonstrated is a manoeuvre to avoid a painful, hideous death. Now you will develop your own along with group formations."

Aarya makes her move, strutting across to a display of weapons on the far wall. Unable to decide, she grabs a fist full of blades and hides them within her outfit. Xander points to Corrina who is now limping.

"Eighteen you're up. Disarm her."

"Are you kidding?" Amani asks. "The moment she grabs a blade Aarya will kill her."

Esmee rolls her eyes at the boy's outburst and flicks back her long, blonde curls. "We can't kill our only hope. Venturers are the future. We're going to teach you to fight or flee, depending on the circumstances."

"I'll flee," says Corrina, checking for bruises.

Beside Corrina, Esmee is a child. Corrina's height and build are twice anything this young Venturer can offer and although her leadership skills shine and her posture is filled with attitude and self-worth, I can tell it's all a character. Our side is weakened but I'd still bet on the inmate.

Amani folds his arms and gestures for Corrina to accept the task.

I raise my arm. "I think it's my turn."

Aarya grins. "The governor killer is eager to die. Fine by me."

We plunge straight into the exercise and circle for a short while, barefoot and bouncing. *Increase your stamina*, I tell myself. Each snatch I try is deflected and after several minutes of lazy attempts, I step away and head to the table myself. Without something to throw, I'm live bait.

"Where are *you* going?"

"Out there I'd be armed," I say, "and I'm not a killer. Last time I checked Czar was still breathing, which is more than they'll say about you when I'm finished."

A toss of the knife from one palm to the other and I remember my first training session. Corrina's eyes brighten when I pick up the pace, dodging and ducking, spinning in smooth spirals to avoid Aarya's persistent kicks. At least someone believes I can defeat this brat, and she doesn't even like me.

Confidence left me years ago but I'm smarter than the Venturers think. A few swings miss my face by millimetres. Adrenaline numbs me against the pain when she does finally strike my jaw. Whistles and hoots sound from the audience but Rae only watches from the sidelines, concerned for us both.

Aarya's brow crinkles and her lip bleeds from a lucky flick of my knife. For every step I take forward she shuffles back. Perhaps I have more influence than predicted.

We both manage to survive the next twenty minutes and escape with a few hot, red grazes and a busted nose. Blood dribbles down my training overalls. It covers them in crimson stains. I can't spare the seconds to wipe my face. Any distraction now could lead to defeat.

Aarya pulls the longest knife from its sheath and twirls the handle in her palm, waiting for a perfect shot. Now my limbs begin to quake and sweat stings my eyes, blinding me. I can't fight somebody I can't see but to survive the session I'll have to.

Behind me, Xander welcomes a male voice that's gruff but familiar. *Warden*. Another spectator to witness my fall.

Energy evaporates from my body; I'm a furnace, producing more water than I can dab away. Aarya isn't phased by the exercise. She just keeps jogging. Is her intention to tire me and outrun me? In the wild, knowing your enemy is stronger gives you two options: run or die. I'll do neither today.

Enough is enough. Warden needs to see my strength.

I stop moving and launch the blade, catching Aarya

off guard and pinning her trouser leg to the wall behind. Gasps and chatters fill the room as Wardrobe discuss my change of attitude but my opponent, for the first time, smiles.

"Congratulations," says Aarya. "Though your aim isn't great, Eden. My heart is here."

"I wasn't aiming for your heart."

I spit blood at Aarya's feet and stalk back to my fellow inmates.

"Body language tells us much about our enemies and you read mine well. Lesson one is complete, I think."

"Lesson? No, that was luck and anger," Corrina interjects.

Aarya yanks the knife free and drops it. She sticks two fingers in the hole of her pants to assess the damage and tuts.

"Why didn't you go for an injury; a real deep, nasty one?"

I shrug. "Can't kill our only hope now, can I? Though I can't say I wasn't tempted to tear off your head."

Two hours later I'm exhausted.

None of us has eaten so we're light headed and grouchy. The blows to my stomach and head still churn the butterflies trapped inside. Unless my colleagues want to witness me vomit it's just not worth the effort.

Warden sits beside me during a hydration break and hands me a tin cup of water, gesturing for me to finish it. We say nothing. Wardrobe is being briefed by the board, learning why mirrors are the ideal protection in a post-apocalyptic world from Xander. I can make out most of their conversation.

"Reflections saved my life hundreds of times," he says. "Mutant intellect is limited so what they see when facing potential food is, instead, themselves. Pocket mirrors are used to check blind corners."

Veil looks disinterested each time Rae nudges him, engrossed in the topic or suggesting ways to improve not only my outfit but theirs from fresh notes and sketches. When we return they'll need ideal protection. I am beginning to see how fragile this group really is but there is something unbelievable about our progress. Not only in our few pitiful days of training but in our friendships. Thrust together on the brink of a disaster forced upon us by Czar, each role has offered to play their part. Rae and Donar's concern for our safety is closely tied to their own and whilst I'm aware there is selfishness in such thoughts, knowing someone else is rooting for you has helped to boost my self-esteem.

Veil, as always, is bored by the ordeal and hasn't given me a second glance since our meet and greet. Why should he? The kid is an ex-Venturer, more than capable of saving himself so by his logic, why bother with the others?

Warden offers a weak smile but has nothing to say to me. I push away the water. I can't trust anything that man has to say or give me, ever. Through my mind flows a vicious idea to leave him behind to rot but as I'm considering such wickedness, clatters and screams sound from outside the training room.

He grabs my arm. "Did you feel that earthquake?"

Pretty big earthquake, I think, but normal or not everyone drops what they're doing. I shake Warden's

Aeon Infinitum: Run For Your Life

hand free and scowl at him. Hurried, cautious gazes meet as the Venturers get their bearings.

My palms are slick and after a few intense minutes my nails have drawn blood I'm clenching so hard. I'm dragged to my feet and pushed forward by Aarya. All three Venturers then run for the weapons rack, clearing it of blades and shields but leaving the inmates unarmed and vulnerable.

"This part of their training?" asks Juliette. "Hey, did you hear me?"

Aarya ignores her and dashes to speak with the other Exigency staff.

Warden releases me and veers off to find his own weapon. My vision blurs as the walls and ceiling begin to vibrate. There's an explosion above us. Rocks and dust rain down, showering us with a layer of thin white powder.

Terrified we'll be buried alive, Aarya swings open the door and grabs a passer-by. Although I can't hear the civilian's story, Aarya's expression tells me the news isn't good. Xander tightens his laces, zips up his jacket and checks the equipment strapped to his belt is in working order. Esmee to does the same.

She shouts, "Breach!"

The Venturers abandon us and spring through the door, leaving Wardrobe and the other inmates to care for ourselves. I scan the room for Warden and call his name but get no response. In the panic, he's slipped out unnoticed and abandoned us. Such behaviour was expected but I'm still surprised and disappointed.

Rae bites her bottom lip and cuddles her sketchbook. "I know what you're thinking, Eden. Don't leave us here, please!"

Donar cradles her and reaches out for me. We all stand bewildered in the centre of the training room.

"Oh, she's not thinking that, don't worry," Juliette assures her.

"I might leave Warden after his disappearing act but I won't leave you. Nobody's coming to save us. Aarya said there was a breach. That means the banished have entered Titan."

Juliette frowns. "Exigency should be on guard!"

"Banished humans frequently enter Titan," Veil says. "Do not look so shocked. I suggest we gather our belongings and head toward the surface. The deeper we flee, the more likely we are to be buried alive."

For once we are without shackles, bars or padlocks. I call for everyone to take hold of another's hand. We've seen the plans and predictions for such an event. Lights will go out. Structures will fall and injure innocent people. Guards will attempt to hold us captive; force us to die with anyone else they deem useless. If we plan to survive this we need Wardrobe's initial designs and a clear path to an emergency exit. At the moment I see neither but I'm not going to let them strike us off.

"Rae, can you lead us to your dorm?" I ask.

She and Donar exchange a worried look. "I think so. The outfits are at Needle and Thread, though, in Sector W. Eden, what about Warden?"

"Not my problem." I usher everyone forward. "Warden only cares about Warden. He's on his own."

Tears stream down Chastity's face who is still clinging helplessly to Donar.

"Eden, are we free now?"

I shrug and gesture for her to get moving. "An open door is enough of an invitation for me, kid."

10

Ginny Bede

Rachana and I huddle together inside somebody's closet in Sector B. After the explosion, she and I dove through an open door and threw ourselves in the safest spot we could find. She's sobbed non-stop for the past three hours and in doing so inhaled several lungs full of dust and debris. The sound of coughing and spluttering invades every pause between each childish whimper.

Banished inmates charged the ark in three waves. First, they hit the barracks, disrupting Venturer training and the rest of Sector C.

Next, a group of twenty or so barged the entrance to Sectors A and B, murdering innocent civilians and emptying our stores of food and warm clothing. The sticky scent of blood fills the air even in our hideout.

Finally, the strongest of their group searched for survivors and are presumably still doing so.

As far as we know, Titan, as it was a day ago, has been lost to an army of inhuman savages. I now understand the meaning of *Ad Initium Děth*.

Revenge would be on my mind too. Their organisational skills are no surprise to me because many of them spoke with Rehab prior to their banishment. Our department has held a deep understanding of what they're feeling for years.

Czar's quarters were their original target based on the path taken. Up two flights of metal steps and down a narrow corridor in Sector F, directly above the Gravitās, delivers them to Titan's unpopular governor and his arrogant council members.

Rachana peers through a crack in the wall. Her vision is relatively clear when the dust begins to settle. Fires set off our forgotten sprinkler system early in the invasion so everything is wet. Floors are slippery and the occasional passers-by struggle to keep their balance. Familiar faces have long since disappeared. Any friends or colleagues I once had are now either dead, hiding or have escaped into the darkness of *Ad Infinitum*. I'm not sure which is crueller.

"Can we make it out of here?" she sniffles, almost reading my mind.

We'll have to stay low and move as fast as our legs can carry the weight If we're going to try. I reach over Rachana and begin cramming clothing from the closet in two of the tenant's abandoned bags. Theft in the ark is punishable by death if you're caught but by now Warden and his guards will be trekking through the wilderness in search of the Harmony Grid several months early.

Upholding the law I doubt will be their priority.

"Nobody's been out so far in the darkness for a long time," I tell her. "I can't tell you with any certainty that we'll succeed."

Rachana wipes her nose on her sleeve. "We can't stay here, Ginny."

"You're right." I sigh, "Follow me and keep quiet."

"Why, where are we going?"

"In search of survivors; anyone who isn't hostile."

Hand-in-hand we tiptoe from the closet and peek into the corridor of sector B. Somewhere in the adjacent sector a woman screams. Gurgles and the clang of cutlery closely follow, then footsteps on the metal floor. They must be raiding the kitchens.

I shove Rachana into an alcove and cover her mouth.

Please run the other way.

I catch a brief glimpse of thick black facial hair and ragged clothing, scarred skin and bare feet. Whoever they are, their needs have exceeded rational behaviour and human emotion. We're dead if they catch us, no matter our reasoning. None of them speaks so I can't be sure they'd understand us if we begged and pleaded anyway.

Mere seconds pass until they leave, yet Rachana and I exhale as though our breaths have been held a century.

I nod once and scurry in the opposite direction toward Wardrobe. Hunting equipment, weapons, medical supplies and suitable footwear are stored there. Perhaps Veil has managed to navigate a clear path, but will he be willing to share guarded supplies?

"I hear voices," says Rachana, tugging my sleeve and nudging closer. "Ginny they're coming. We have to hide. Let's go back."

Wardrobe's front office door is unlocked. I point, hold a finger to my mouth, and urge her forward. Rachana swings it open and slips inside. Banished inmates may still remember the layout of Titan and will head our way for weapons but when they do, I'll be waiting.

"In here," says one of the voices.

"Rae? Rae it's Ginny."

I take a few anxious steps forward and reach out, unable to see much in the lingering smoke. There are muttering and whispers but sure enough, it's Veil, followed by his trainee Wardrobe assistants Rae and Donar and their inmates.

I divert my gaze to some of the other faces with rags to their mouths. "Where'd *you* come from?"

"Sector C caved in on us during training. Czar's Venturers abandoned us to deal with the breach. They never came back," Juliette says. "Are you alone?"

I lead them toward the office door and tap to warn Rachana. When we enter she's hunched behind a desk.

"What are you all doing here?" she asks.

Eden, whom I haven't seen in months, shoves me aside and begins scrambling through items of clothing and fabric at the far end. Elvandra chases after her and rummages until they find something similar to the pictures she's holding. The others from Wardrobe look tired and are coughing.

"Donar, I can't find your designs," says Elvandra, waving at him.

"I didn't finish them," he gasps between each laboured breath. "Sorry Chastity. Get Eden to find something for you and Corrina."

The young blonde rubs her eyes and dashes to help the others. Eden hands her a pair of boots and a long coat. It's far too big but well padded and warm. Corrina opts for fur.

"You're going outside," I say. "Got anything over

there for Rachana?"

Eden nods and throws some dark coloured fabric at Rachana's feet. She inspects it, wraps it around her body then ties the material with some rope. Fashion isn't important now, I remind myself, and then help her cover any remaining patches of exposed skin.

Another few hours pass before we're equipped and ready to go. The corridors are beginning to quiet but smoke from the ruins seeps beneath the door, slowly choking us.

Veil scavenged what little food remained in the kitchen during our dress-up, but if we are to survive out there some of us will need weapons as well as scraps.

"Where have you all been for three hours?" I ask Amani.

"Hiding in the dorms until it was safe and we could make a run for supplies."

Eden throws me some extra clothing. I tug on the jumper and thick socks but I'm still shivering. The breach must be close, letting in the freezing air. Everyone huddles together.

"Survival is impossible out there," says Corrina. "Look at us. We'll never make it. We should have followed the Venturers in training earlier."

"You're welcome to stay behind," says Eden, breaking from the group. "Venturers may have experience but they're reckless and cocky. Besides, they took off in a flash and clearly didn't want us tagging along; they thought we'd get them killed. Rae, where are the weapons?"

"The armoury." Elvandra points to locked double doors at the back of the room. "The key is in that office.

None of us is firearms trained though."

"I am," Veil says.

Eden retrieves the key and scurries through a passage leading to the armoury. When she returns, Veil is given a sickle, carefully crafted and it appears, antique.

"Even with blunt museum pieces?"

"I can manage," he says.

"Basic training taught me enough," Eden says. "Most of the rifles probably won't work anyway and the blades are dull. Still, I'd rather have something to swing than nothing but my bare hands."

Veil nods in agreement. "I cannot feed us with this," he says, then his lips upturn slightly. "You are fortunate I prefer to hunt people, anyway."

"And the manoeuvre training we're all lacking?" asks Amani, scowling at the battle-scarred teen reaper. "How important was *that* lesson?"

Eden sighs. "A monkey can dance and dodge, Amani. Training isn't necessary. We'll improvise. Everybody ready?"

"As I'll ever be," I reply, gesturing at Rachana to gather her things.

Two damp lines cut the filth on her cheeks and disappear beneath her clothing. I dig deep into my pocket, take out my canteen and offer it to her. Rae dabs at Rachana's dirty face with a tissue, gentle and silent as a mouse as the kid unscrews the lid to smell the contents.

She grimaces. "Ale, *now*?"

"Hold on to it for me," I tell her, leading her to Juliette's side and joining their hands. "I can't leave here without Mitchell."

Juliette glares at me. "You're not serious? Ginny, don't leave her with me!"

"I have to. He's my brother," I reason. "You'd do the same."

Rae stashes the remaining tissues in Rachana's pocket. "Did you even train her, Ginny?"

"I'll be ok," Rachana says between sniffles.

"I doubt it'll matter," says Donar, tugging on an extra layer of clothing and a hat. "I worked for a few years in maintenance. I know Titan's tunnels. I'm coming with you, for Pagen."

Elvandra takes a step back and scowls. "Pagen's dead, Donar. Don't be a fool. You're not staying in this tomb, that's ridiculous. Flona's dead already, I'm sure. She wouldn't want me risking my life. Come with us, please."

Donar tugs Elvandra from the others, lowers his voice and embraces her. For a while, they remain connected and her shoulders shake as she sobs against his chest. Then Donar releases his friend and nods at the exit. Rae creeps back to the kid, nudges her, and retrieves a tissue for herself. Desperate not to leave him, she pleas one final time but is once again rejected. I'd never have deemed Wardrobe colleagues such close friends, but misery loves company.

"Everything all right?" I ask as she passes me.

Elvandra nods and ushers Juliette and Rachana to the door, then glances back one last time at Donar and me.

"Ginny, I hope you find your brother." She leans forward and kisses my cheek. "In the meantime, please take care of mine."

Then she smiles, picks up her weapon, and the group follow Eden to what they pray will be freedom. When the door swings closed behind them, Donar clears his throat and raises an eyebrow. He holds out an arm, suggesting I be the first to leave our little sanctuary.

"Shall we?"

Besides a thick smog that is displaced by a cold breeze every now and then, the corridors of Titan are empty and silent. Eden and her group must have already cleared this sector, heading for the bay they shoved Veil's banishment group in, prompting his requirement for robes in the first place. Working in Rehab, you learn these things from an inmate's file. If he's leading them it's where they'll be heading, giving me some confidence they'll be free of Titan's boundaries soon. It also gives us a location to head for after retrieving Mitchell.

As I try to block out the thoughts of Rachana crossing such torturous terrain with men and women she barely knows or trusts, I allow my mind to wander.

Civilised humans haven't mixed for over six hundred years with the Earth's surface and most of what we'd recognise as familiar has been long since destroyed. Buildings, schools and hospitals, for example, were amongst the first structures to be torn down during the panic. Civilians were so desperate for food, warmth and companionship that almost anyone openly living by comfortable means was swarmed within the first month. Of course, those who chose to wait out the ordeal in the sanctuary of their own homes were, later, driven insane when their relatives starved to death or froze in the darkness, goaded to creep out in search of something–*anything*– to feed their children. I can only hope if they make it someplace safe that they rebuild a society with more common sense this time.

"Do you think they'll make it?" I whisper.

Donar shudders. "Don't ask me questions you don't want the answer to, Ginny. "

Donar may not wish to discuss such facts, but before Eden's imprisonment, she and I often picked conversation about NORA. Our seasons ceased to exist, plunging half the planet into darkness for six months and the other into a constant summer. Sweltering heat, barren wastelands with little or no vegetation, droughts and as you can imagine, creatures so used to being cooked alive they've been driven mad; crazed with thirst and in agonizing pain.

On the opposite end of this scale, anything outside for more than a couple of minutes, if not fully clothed and stocked with supplies, is dead. The Earth is snow-covered, thick to the knees in some places and frozen solid in others. Animals suited to such conditions have migrated and hunt what remains of humanity, however, mutated from the destruction of nuclear plants in past years. Survivors are brutal, psychotic Cannibals who wait for their regular release of banished inmates like school children would wait for a dinner bell.

Unless you live between the two, you're either a meal or a monster.

I allow Donar to pass me and together we sneak side-by-side along the walls, halting to peer around corners using Wardrobe's hand-held mirrors and then jog on the tips of our toes as not to draw too much attention.

There's an explosion above us and the ceiling cracks, showering us in fine white dust and kick-starting my feet to a sprint in any direction that isn't blocked with rubble or bodies. I draw a blade from my belt and cover my face with my free hand to mask the scent of charred flesh.

Donar gestures at the living quarters and, using his shoulder, thrusts a dented door off its hinges and falls forward. I aid him to a stance and together we sneak between items strewed along the floor. Mattresses, canned food, broken furniture, body parts and paperwork. The stench, although unbearable, is intoxicating and boosts our adrenaline.

"Where do we start?" Donar asks, pointing at the several options ahead leading to various areas of our living quarters.

I gesture in the direction of the tavern. "That way."

"Really?"

To the right are bedrooms and bathrooms and to the left, the canteen and sports facilities. I remember the last time Mitchell and I spoke and turn left, heading for his favourite place.

"Mitch and I are too alike for our own good. Trust me, if he's alive, he'll be there."

11

Eden Maas

The silo is abandoned.

Veil is the first to enter, blade at shoulder height, although he still holds little confidence it'll kill anything- stun perhaps. On *Ad Infinitum* only when something is one hundred percent dead can you relax.

At the entrance to the silo, Donar's mentor Juliette decides to take her chances and search for her family. Chastity begins to cry and urges us not to separate. There is safety in numbers so I remind her the structure isn't secure and she'll be crushed. Desperate to save them she sets off regardless and I know as she rounds the corner that I will never see her again.

Still cradling her designs to her chest, Rae moves behind Veil and ahead of me, sandwiched in the safest spot for protection and escape, but she's crying over Juliette which will draw attention. If Veil goes down she can outrun me and still survive so I envy her, but in favour of my reputation I grind my teeth and glare at her back, studying each flinch, whimper and cower to learn as much about her fears and instincts as possible. If we're caught in an unfortunate fight, likely to end in death for the majority, I need to be sure she'll have my back and if not I should be sure to avoid her clumsy attempts to swing a blade.

Basic training might have highlighted my weaknesses but on the inside, it's reinforced my strengths and thickened my skin in the process. I'm prepared to lose this group to radiation, mutants or starvation but I'm concerned about losing Warden. He and I were partners.

Daemon Czar, after taking the throne from his cancer-ridden father, was beginning to grind everyone's bones with the introduction of sharper food rations, longer working hours and almost pointless wages. I'd had enough; Warden and I decided to end the reign and free our people, giving them an opportunity to break out of Titan as a community and expand during the daylight, then slip beneath to hibernate through the darkness. Warden denied all possibilities of the assassination failing. He'd take Czar to a meeting and there I'd pierce his heart, bringing the government down with him.

I'd been too eager to complete our business and with shaking hands, I missed the target. Czar was injured but I didn't stick around long enough to see blood.

Warden's eyes widened and he fell to Czar's side. I ran. Whilst skidding around the final corner, merely a finger's wriggle away from the next sector, a guard grabbed my shoulders and pinned me to the ground. Together he and a colleague dragged me to an interrogation room and knowing I had absolutely no chance of escaping the death sentence, Warden pulled his men away and ordered they stand down.

"Found a new favourite, Warden?" the guard joked and slapped me hard on the backside before exiting the room.

I glared after him. "I'm prepared to pay the price for us both."

Warden loosened my cuffs and slid a tin cup of water across the desk for me.

"Drink, you might not get anything for a while."

I shook my head. "Let them kill me. If you involve yourself any more they'll figure out we're more than acquaintances and you'll be strung up beside me. Deny all knowledge, Warden. It's fine, I can handle this."

Without saying a word, Warden smiled and strode from the room, slamming the door behind him. The water swayed in the cup. Dry from arguing I wet my tongue enough to prepare a further argument but was rendered unconscious before I'd planned my next move.

Drugs were a sneaky trick I should never have fallen for. Of course, Warden wasn't going to kill me or let anyone else do so. What was I thinking?

I imagine the way I feel about his missing presence in the silo is exactly how Warden felt faced with my execution. Suddenly I'm less guilty about wanting to find him and eager to do for him what he did for me. If he left with the Venturers, slid out and abandoned me, there *must* have been a good reason.

"Veil, I can't do this."

The others freeze and throw themselves against the wall. My voice is louder than I intended so I hush their whines, hand them my pack and before I can move but two steps, Veil's nails are in my flesh.

"Are you insane?"

"What? *No*. I can't just leave him. Let me go."

"He is halfway across the Harmony Grid by now,

and so should we be."

Chastity whimpers. "Are you leaving us too?"

"*Nobody* is leaving," says Corrina. "Eden, whoever you're chasing can't be worth your life. We *need* you."

"I doubt it."

"Of the group you and Veil are our only chance at survival out there. Veil's an experienced Venturer and you, well, sorry honey but your heart is iron. I've no doubt should any of us become sick or injured you'd vote to leave us for bait or murder us yourself, but beneath the evil I see a real leader. We can't make it on our own." Her voice breaks. "Please, Eden."

Veil hushes us; we duck and pin our bodies to the wall, watching as a pair of ugly mutants slump by. My eyes widen at their disgusting appearance. Their hair is patchy and thin, revealing red sores at the backs of their necks and ears. The tallest is limping and I see a misshapen chunk of his left leg is missing from a bite. His clothing hangs loose, revealing his buttocks. Across his stomach there's thick fur which pokes beneath a blood-stained shirt. But he has that unusual firefly glow to his skin, just like Veil said.

It's clear they aren't with the banished inmates, but I wish both sides luck in their private battle for Titan's resources.

"Those are not inmates," Veil says, deep in thought. "I wonder-"

"No time to wonder," I reply. "Can you get them out of here?"

Corrina shakes me and lowers her voice. "Think of Chastity and Rae. The Harmony Grid might hold a future for them and you're willing to dispose of that for a *memory."*

"He's not a memory. He saved my life; I should return the favour," I say through grinding teeth.

"Elvandra saved your life, *not* Warden. Those designs she's carrying are far more than just colours on a bit of parchment. Right there is your existence. You're wearing it. If not for Elvandra and Veil you'd have been kicked out of here without a chance or a name. She routed for you." Corrina points to Elvandra who is hunkered low beneath layer upon layer of clothing, petrified. "Look at her face, Eden."

I flinch and grab Veil's blade, whipping it around to meet her throat and hold it there. Our eyes lock as we stand stone still.

The smallest mutant halts and lifts his wide nostrils to the air, sniffing for any sign of life. I hold my breath and dare not even blink. With any luck, the smoke will have masked our scent.

"Is this mystery man worth her death?" she says, shaking.

Her eyes drift and catch sight of the mutant retreating to join his friend and seeing his hideous reflection in her eyes, the two of us relax. Cowering, Rae slips passed and stands with Amani and Rachana. Chastity, now alone, can't peel her eyes from the blood that's beginning to coat my blade. If I press any harder I'll kill her.

"Now, thanks to you," says Corrina, "every critter and bone-cruncher on this planet is going to smell my blood. May as well butcher and serve me up early. If it'll help your cause I could scream."

I lower the blade and hand it to Veil. "Guard that

thing better. Next time you insult me I'll take off your face."

Pleased with myself I shove her aside. If Warden chose to leave me at the most crucial of times then perhaps Corrina is right anyway. Maybe he *doesn't* deserve my time and, certainly, he can't take my friends'.

"Carry on, Eden," Veil says, scowling, "and you will be needing a hood of your own sooner than you think."

12

Ginny Bede

It feels as though my heart has imploded when my eyes rest upon my brother's lifeless corpse.

Donar's palm meets my shoulder and together we stand in silence for several minutes before the tears begin to stream and the weight of reality knocks the air from my lungs. I slide down the open door frame and linger on the balls of my feet until they ache. After a few attempts at lifting me and being shoved aside, Donar grows tired of my self-pity and hauls me up.

"He's dead, mate. Nothing you can do now. Let's catch up with the others."

"I can't, I have to bury him."

"We can't coordinate a funeral during an apocalypse."

Donar shoves me against the wall and cuts off my air supply with the back of his arm. I shuffle and squirm to break free but I'm pinned.

"I said I'd help find him to honour my own brother. Now if you want to join Mitchell in the six-foot hole you're planning to dig, be my guest. I'll be damned if I allow your idiocy to force my fate too."

Donar releases me and I gasp, then throw my body

across a table to get as far from his strength as possible. My throat is raw and my skin already bruised.

"You're a maniac." I cough. "Where's your humanity?"

"Out there." Donar slams the door shut and makes his way toward Mitchell's body. "I'm not usually a violent man, Ginny, but Mitch wouldn't want you risking more lives for the sake of his physical state. His soul left this pit when whatever creature did that to him entered it. Find reassurance that he's somewhere peaceful."

Donar turns Mitch over and despite the injury which I have no doubt killed him, I see the effects of his alcoholism on his frame. He's thin, withdrawn cheekbones and crooked teeth. His eyes were dim before death; I can't believe I allowed such a deterioration. Why hadn't I intervened? There's a pain in my chest I'm unable to contain and I gesture at Ginny to cover his face then sob into my coat. His final scream was preserved just for me. Am I being punished for rejecting him?

"Pain keeps us moving, Ginny," he continues. "Harness it. I'm not trying to be cruel but we've got to get out of here. The place is crumbling and on fire. Think of Rachana; leaving Mitch behind means you can save the girl's life." Donar holds out his palm and smiles. "Now are you with me or what?"

I creep toward my brother, hopeful that he thought to bring his wallet despite usually drinking for free. Inside I'll find a picture of our family when Mitch and I were kids. A kind reminder of childhood innocence and forgotten hope. To avoid seeing his twisted expression, I turn my head away and fish in every pocket to pull out a battered, ale-stained wallet. I plant a kiss firmly on it and hide it in my coat.

"Ok, I'm ready," I say.

Together we jog back down the hall and out toward Veil's silo.

Smoke fills many of the rooms now and the maintenance lights are beginning to flicker, indicating the generators are unmanned and require refuelling. Most of Titan is lit with candles or torches, but some sectors require brighter lights to function. Usually, I'd offer to help the engineers, given that their boss– an old, grey guy named Bert- once distracted Czar's guards long enough for me to carry Mitchell home. I hope Bert escaped unscathed.

We round the corner without trouble, coming up on the silo's entrance and through the haze I catch a glimpse of Veil's lowered hood. Donar and I bolt to meet them, wondering why they hadn't made a move sooner. I prepare to scold Rachana; if they're waiting because she didn't want to leave me behind I'll kill her myself.

On approach, we slow and are met by raised firearms and terrified faces until Elvandra wraps her arms around Donar and squeezes him.

"Where's Juliette?" I ask.

Eden rolls her eyes and gestures for Chastity and Corrina to help us with our gear. Chastity grabs one of my bags and Corrina one of mine from Wardrobe. Veil sheaths his blade.

"Dead probably." Veil shrugs, "My sympathies."

"What happened?" asks Donar.

"Juliette wanted to find her family," Amani replies. "Sorry Donar, I know you were friends."

We pause for a while, watching mutants dash in

empty-handed and return with stolen clothing, canned food and the remaining weapons. Veil holds us steady with an extended arm and, when the silo is finally silent, we sprint for the night sky.

It doesn't take long until I'm out of breath and beginning to feel a sharp stabbing pain in my side. Veil shoves me hard from behind. I'm thankful for his previous experience and large ego. Even more so when Chastity slips and renders herself unconscious on the concrete floor. Despite Eden, Corrina and Rae remaining oblivious, their focus solely on the exit, Veil scoops her up and runs with the kid slumped over his shoulder. I had never taken him for a hero but today I am thankful he's here and been through all this once before.

A blaring alarm sounds. Blue and red lights flash, distorting our view. The noise of cranking stone cogs shocks my eardrums. Veil is screaming and pointing ahead of us but I can't make out what he's saying. I follow his gesture and see the silo's door is falling. If we don't pick up the pace we're either going to be crushed or buried alive.

Veil hands me the young inmate then pushes us forward even though he's heading the wrong way toward a maintenance desk. I can't help but continue running now there's another life under my care but I don't want to leave anyone behind.

Chastity groans. "What's going on?"

I pat her legs. "You're fine, we're going to make it. Try to stay awake."

Veil skids to a stop beside a large metal counter that's gleaming with tools the size of my arm. They must be for maintaining the external doors and harvesters.

Veil's face is pink and his cheeks are puffed from the weight of the oversized screwdriver he rests across his shoulders. Sweat soaks his neck and blinds him, but still the teenage saviour powers on.

Eden, Rae and Corrina dash beneath the doors with only a few feet remaining. Rachana and Amani stand behind them, waving frantically for me to hurry. I'm tiring and already know Chastity and I are dead. Veil manages to overtake us and props the tool beneath the door just in time to jam it with a metre or so to spare, giving me chance to roll the girl under and then shimmy beneath it myself. Once safe I turn to see the tool bending beneath the door's weight and when I turn back I'm hit with freezing air, seeing nothing but my iced breath before me in laboured puffs. It feels like I'll never breathe easy again.

"*What* were you thinking?" Donar heaves. He's hunched over, resting on his knees to catch a breath. "Veil, you could've been killed!"

"Yet I am alive." He nudges me. "Saved your ass."

"And gave every mutant on the planet access to Titan," says Eden, shaking her head. "Just because you've done this before, Veil, doesn't give you the right to abandon us. Sorry, Ginny, but I'd have written you off there."

"Careful with the affection, Twelve," I sigh, "but yeah, me too."

Veil grumbles. "It seems the only reason you appreciate me is because I will keep you alive."

Elvandra kneels by my side and helps me remain steady whilst Rachana gives Chastity a tight hug. I'm so pleased to see them that I forget to ask why they delayed their escape to begin with. Were Donar and I faster at finding Mitchell than we thought? Had Veil delayed their escape?

Eden answers my questions with a simple, terrifying statement.

"We weren't raided by banished inmates at all, were we?"

I shake my head free of snowflakes and scowl. "*What?*"

"We were delayed because the silo was filled with mutants stealing things from Titan. *Mutants!* Intelligent, opposable thumb possessing, communicating animals," she says.

Rachana's eyes widen. "I was right, Ginny!"

"I agree it is odd, but we should let the beasts take whatever they want. Czar got a head start and did not deem any of Titan's assets worth saving or he would have ordered a squad to round up extra supplies," Veil says. "It matters not who began this war, only who finished it."

"We aren't at war," Eden replies, "are we?"

"Who cares? You're not suggesting Czar left on his own, without food and water?" asks Corrina, her arms folded. "He's dumb but not suicidal."

Veil shrugs. "Someone initiated the seal of this silo. I cannot imagine they would lock themselves inside after the collapse. Now we are out we should find somewhere to hide for a few hours and regain our strength. I cannot tell you how far into winter we are so let us function on the assumption we have endless months of this to survive." Veil nods in my direction. "You did good, Ginny."

I force a smile. "You too, kid."

Eden grabs her things and sets off across the potato plantation. Ahead by approximately half a mile, Titan's boundary ends and is protected by a tall metal fence and a now abandoned watch tower.

"We should climb high and fast if we want to survive. I saw what those things did to our neighbours and I'm *not* going to be dessert." Eden spins and opens her arms. "Well, anyone else want to live?"

"Eden's right," says Rachana, taking hold of my hand and pulling me lazily along. "We saw and heard the destruction. Banished inmates or not, so far we've survived because of luck and The Hood, which *isn't* a compliment."

Veil nods. "I never expected one."

Amani rolls his eyes. "We're on our own and right now, Eden and Veil are our best chances." He scans the sky and huddles deeper into his layers of clothing. "I think there's going to be a storm. That tower has a roof and a rope ladder we can pull up behind us. I vote we follow Twelve."

"A storm? How can you tell?" Chastity asks.

"Before my sentence I worked in Expediency. I was a trainee weather analyst."

Already there's a fresh layer of white powder beneath our feet and our boots crumple it as we trek along toward the watchtower, taking Amani's word for it. Elvandra and Chastity are close behind Eden, followed by Donar, Amani, Veil and I. Corrina labours behind us, fascinated by the shadows cast by nearby trees and lurking predators.

"Eighteen, curiosity is a killer," I remind her. "Can I

help you with those bags?"

Her brown eyes narrow as she cracks her knuckles and shakes her head. It's clear how uncomfortable the weight of her clothes and supplies are making her; although she's athletic and determined, her voice strains. I can't force her to accept help, though.

"Ginny, we're not safe anywhere out here, least of all that tower."

"If you believe that, why follow us?" I ask.

"We're in this together," Corrina murmurs. "Besides, I need to be sure the kid survives to prove Twelve wrong. From the start she didn't believe Warden would allow Chastity to live. She thinks if we make it across this Harmony Grid he'll either kill or banish her. Eden said we'd be kinder to just-" Her voice breaks and she shakes her head. "Never mind, we should catch up to the others."

At the base of the watchtower my stomach churns. It's much higher than I'd judged from the silo's exit and having lived underground and enclosed all my life, heights and I aren't the greatest of friends. Rachana shoots straight up the ladder and barely blinks, then stares down at us with a smile on her face.

"Been up here before," she reminds me.

"It's a ladder, not a snake," I tell myself and get a snort of a laughter from Eden.

Veil hauls me up the gap between the ground and the first rung and from there on, I'm alone. My palms are sweaty despite the ice and the ladder swings with every step, making me nauseous. I'm blinded by fear and before I register exactly how much of Titan's grounds you can see from the top, I've made it. Rachana sits beside me and we wait patiently whilst Chastity- whose training proved her resilience to heights- Elvandra, Veil, Amani and Eden follow.

As I gather the courage to peer over the edge, from the tree line where the fence is down, bolts a creature of unimaginable size. Its body is covered in matted grey hair with paws the size of my face and gleaming white teeth. It moves swiftly across the snow, leaving a trail of blood and filth behind it. All four legs are thick with muscle and no doubt flea-infested.

Corrina, now on the second rung of the ladder, catches a glimpse of the beast and, fighting the weight of her gear, struggles to pick up the pace. I scream at her to drop her gear and climb to safety. We can worry about our stock later.

"Do something," Rachana urges. "Somebody lower me down, I'm light. I'll help her."

"Absolutely not," says Veil.

Eden snipes. "*I'll* go."

Elvandra grips her jacket. "We need you. If you die we're all screwed."

Chastity folds her knees to her chest and covers her ears in time to stifle Corrina's scream. There's a short cry for help, a gurgle and a squelch as the beast rips into her flesh. After a distant howl, the creature takes off with the bottom half of Corrina's body still in its jaw. When Veil peers over the edge, the end of the ladder is missing and entwined around the rest are Eighteen's upper remains. Her eyes are open and her mouth agape.

"Eden," he says, motioning to the hatch. "Take a look."

She flinches and covers her mouth. "Veil, why

would you-"

"That is the sight of your promotion. One inmate dies and another replaces her."

Eden punches Veil hard in the shoulder, knocking him off balance and onto his backside. A disgusted, terrified silence settles among our group. If we continue to lose members, soon we will be alone or dead ourselves. There's safety in numbers and whilst we're in this tower the beast can't reach us. So I hope.

"Do you want another scar, Veil?" Eden asks, her eyes unblinking. "I'm sure I can find somewhere to stab you! I've had practice."

"There's nothing we can do now. She's dead," says Donar. "Wardrobe have the map Zthora presented us with during the briefing. We should plan a route out of here before that thing comes back for more."

"Ginny, how far is it across the grid?" asks Elvandra, shuffling to sit beside me with tears welling in her eyes.

"You have the map, *right*?" Eden snaps. When I cringe, the inmate slams her fist against the wooden floor and growls. "Goddamn it! Please don't tell me our only map is in *her* bag."

"Sorry, Twelve, she took it from me in the silo. I offered to carry the bags but she wouldn't let me." I hold up my hands. "Plus side, though. It's still hanging there. One of us should climb down."

"Stubborn brute," Eden snipes, muttering under her breath about the responsibility once again being left to her. "This is just typical. *Ooh, perhaps we should sit this thing out together and save the girl*," she mocks. "Yeah, look where that got you! Guts all sprayed across the snow and the map is probably torn in half. Course, it'll be the half we need that got eaten instead of your big head."

The group back away, half expecting Eden to hold one of us hostage or offer us up to save her own skin. But she never looks back, just continues to yell at the body.

Unafraid and filled with fury, Eden clambers clumsily down the top few rungs, wraps her ankle around one and tugs it for security, then releases her top half. Now upside down Eden rifles through Corrina's bags until she finds the folded parchment, then pockets it. She's still cursing when she re-emerges and huddles, miserably, in the corner. Her complexion is almost green.

"Eden, we can bury her when we-"

Eden holds up her hand to cut my offer short.

Donar crawls beside her and runs his fingers through her midnight locks. Coated in dust, ash, a light layer of snow and now the blood of her fellow inmate, Twelve begins to cry.

"*Here*," she sniffles, handing the map to Donar. "If anyone else wants to die, crack on. I didn't even like her but I'm not sure how much longer I can take this shit."

13

Elvandra Rae

I'm surprised how quickly Veil and Eden fall asleep after Corrina's death. Unfortunately for me, I'm much less able to forget the sound of gnawing fangs. Just knowing I'll be forced to climb passed her remains within the next few hours curdles my blood.

"Can't sleep?"

Rachana approaches the ledge and rests her arms on the barrier, then allows her chin to sit comfortably upon them. In the moonlight, her red hair is almost alight and her eyes burn with curiosity as they scan the landscape. Howls, roars and the occasional distant screech are carried with the wind and in the distance, we spot smoke from several campfires, which I'm sure are no longer manned. If they are it's by the ghosts of the mutants' latest victims.

"We need a lookout," I tell her.

"*You?*" Her eyebrows raise. "Rather Veil, or Ginny."

I shrug. "They're sleeping. Ginny hates heights and Veil needs his strength if he's going to lead us."

"Got to admit," she says. "I feel sorry for him being forced outside again. The darkness is-" Rachana pauses, shudders and stands upright. "Consuming."

"He's our best hope though," I tell her. "Wait, did you see that?"

Down by the tree line beyond the collapsed fence is a continually moving shadow in the shape of a humanoid. Rachana nods and grunts, seemingly uninterested.

"Been there for a while," she says. "Don't worry, from what I gather they can't climb. I've been watching them attempt the trees; there are few creatures I've identified so far who know what their limbs are for." Rachana forces a smile and gives me a light pat on the shoulder. "Is it true you worked in Wardrobe?" Fascinated by the shadows I can only nod. "Eden was yours, wasn't she? I mean, when Warden planned for them to check out the grid and return with some news. She's so strong, I can't imagine her not returning with anything but positive details of a new sanctuary."

I hum. "She's a treat all right. An attempted murderer, did you know?"

Rachana smiles. "In her eyes it's clear. She's filled with such spite. She wanted to go back for Warden, did you hear her in the silo?"

Together we glance at a sleeping Eden, squashed beneath Chastity and Donar. Her eyelids flicker as she dreams and her black hair blows gently in the snowy breeze. If she's troubled by anything but our current situation, her sleep sure isn't affected.

"Warden visited her cell often too. One of the guards told me. I think they were friends." I explain. "He introduced us but not without warning me how vicious and unforgiving she can be. Personally, I don't see the malicious nature he spoke of. I see survival instincts and anger."

I hand Rachana the drawings of Eden's Venturing costume and as she holds the top, I unravel the parchment. There are a few sketches on the page but in the centre is the splodge of green I used to convince Veil back at Wardrobe.

"Donar wasn't ready to run," I say, "especially once he learned Chastity was his assignment. Those guys back in Wardrobe's management said the inmates should explore every point on the map with the help of trained and experienced Venturers."

Rachana peeks over at the blonde inmate of an innocent fourteen years of age and no doubt feels for her. Neither of us can remember the crimes she committed, if any, but we both agree a girl so young can only be destroyed in prison.

"How about you?" I ask.

"Ginny became my boss when I lost my parents."

"What happened to them? A problem shared is a-"

"Convincing me isn't necessary. Now we're out of Titan, I'm more than happy to tell you." Rachana takes a deep breath before beginning her tale. "Czar was so frightened of Titan's walls being penetrated from the outside, but by worrying so much he forgot about their knowledge. These people, the criminals they decided to release rather than murder, remembered from working here how to gain access to Titan through the maintenance tunnels, caves and wells. Gradually they slipped back inside without getting caught, learned to live outside Warden's radar and integrated themselves. I," she says, closing her eyes, "am the product of such success."

Rachana gestures at her pack and I pass it over, careful not to drop it over the edge. From the front pocket she pulls a folding knife and flicks it open. In the palm of her hand, Rachana cuts a straight line and allows the blood to drop beneath the wooden slats of the watchtower. Without realising, she's advertising our whereabouts by scent but she continues nevertheless. Before I can gasp, Rachana wipes the remaining blood on her coat and holds up her palm.

"I don't understand. You're *healed?*"

Rachana hushes me. "Not all mutants are bad, Elvandra. My father was a banished inmate and survived outside for six months, the same time period the venture had been planned for. When he returned my mother found him hiding and kept him safe. Harbouring a fugitive is punishable by death, like a lot of other things in Titan, but bravery consumed her. That and the love she felt for the injured survivor. I don't know why I heal so well; it's the only perk I have. Perhaps because my father's body adapted to the intense change in lifestyle."

"So you're a mutant?"

"Of sorts. Ginny knows, I think. He's smarter than we give him credit for I'm sure. After all, he judges people for a living to find their faction." She sighs. "Please don't advertise it. The less suspicious people are, the less likely I am to be assassinated or something." Rachana gestures at Eden. "If it's my life versus hers? *Hmm*, I may heal quickly but resurrection is yet to be tested."

14

Eden Maas

Even the mornings are dark.

I wake to a navy canvas, half-hidden beneath the blonde hair of my fellow inmate. Veil is awake and standing beside Rachana and Elvandra who were up during the night whispering about shadows in the woods. Through the incoming storm's wind and cries of distant mutant creatures, their words weren't clear.

Beneath us lingers the stench of rotting flesh. Being in a tiny cell with my own filth for months seems to have prepared me but for the others, I'm not so sure. Donar stirs and in doing so wakes up the kid who begins to cry when she catches sight of Corrina's body.

"We can't leave her there," Chastity mutters. "It's inhumane."

I tell her, "It's the only option."

I hop to my feet and brush down my several layers of clothing. Beneath the first jumper- a khaki green itchy nightmare- I'm beginning to sweat, but there's no way I'm unravelling my padding. If that beast comes back I need to be protected and prepared for survival.

"Eden, what's your problem?" Donar asks, pulling the kid to his side and stroking her hair. "She's just a girl."

"She's an *inmate*," I correct, "and her number was four, meaning there are three other women in there she's more dangerous than. Think about that. Her cute button nose may fool you but how likely are those mutant monstrosities to stop and say *aww*?"

"They're not inside anymore, Eden. Just like us their plans were disrupted and if we don't move it soon, we'll be dead. Then none of us can complain or poke fun at *anyone* anymore," Donar replies. "If Chastity wants to move Corinna's remains, who are we to stop her?"

"We are the people who are going to get beheaded helping her," Veil intervenes.

I exhale with relief. "The time for giving in to emotion has passed." I soften, "I'm sorry she died. Corrina thought a lot about you; routed for you to stay alive. She begged me in training to hide you so Czar and Warden couldn't force you on their pathetic life-saving quest. I guess either way you're on your own now."

"Nobody's on their own," says Elvandra. Our eyes meet for a moment before she rubs her face, defeated. "We shouldn't fight amongst ourselves," she continues. "We're all going to make it across the grid. Nobody else is going to die and if I have to move Corinna's remains from that ladder before Chastity will climb down then so be it."

I must roll my eyes because Donar is on me again.

"Hey, for now we're willing to put your selfish behaviour behind us and work as a team. I don't know about anyone else in this tower but my goodwill can only last so long. Warden's gone, Corrina's dead, Juliette abandoned us and we'll perish too if we keep yelling at one another."

"I'm far from selfish. Got you all this far, didn't I?"

"With help," Veil states.

"Sure, with your help, Veil. You all said it yourselves we're your biggest hope."

I inhale, close my eyes, and try with all my might to cage my temper. I don't want to lose control. These people trust me and despite my need to be independent and self-sufficient, I'm growing to like them.

"How did we end up here?" Amani asks, shuddering between each word. "It's hopeless."

Donar gives him a reassuring pat on the back. "It worked out for the best, actually."

"Oh yeah, like how?" I snipe.

"If not for the outsiders bursting in and disrupting life, you'd all be on your own and we'd still be stuck inside. Least here we're together and for now, safe," Donar replies.

"Tell Corrina that," I say, swallowing hard. "Enough of this. I'll go first, untangle her body and lower her to the ground as humanely as possible. I'm *not* going to stick around and bury her. In this weather, she'll only freeze and if I'm being honest, the time for respect and honour passed when she got bit in half."

Veil nods and moves out of my way. "Fine."

"Veil will throw your pack down when you're safe and then send the others down one by one. He can be the last," Donar says, eyeing Chastity.

"I will not leave anyone weaker than I up here alone, especially if I cannot get back up." Veil's hood goes up. "Ready, Twelve?"

"As I'll ever be."

I back down the ladder, swaying as little as my body can manage to prevent motion sickness, then as before I hang upside down to untie the remains of my fellow inmate. Her body thumps to the ground and I cringe, glancing back up at Chastity whose eyes are squeezed shut.

"See anything else?" Veil asks.

I shake my head and continue down the ladder. Once I'm dangling from the final rung, Veil gives me the thumbs up and shouts that the landscape is clear. For now, we're mutant free. The others follow one by one and those after throw down their bags, each caught carefully to avoid losing the contents or damaging our packs. If one of the water bottles bursts or a weapon misfires, we're done for. Both complete opposites and both equally as devastating to suffer the consequences of. Personally, I'd be rather be shot than die of thirst.

I drag Corrina as far from the watchtower as possible and hide her body beneath some bushes, hoping the animals will leave her to rest in peace. Chastity's eyes follow us and when I return, she bears a tiny smile and nods to thank me. Instead of acknowledging it I barge passed and take the lead toward the fence. Now is a safe time to make haste for the collapsed fence and venture into the wild, following the others.

We're not out of the compound long before we're huddled like potatoes in a sack. The lack of personal space is beginning to grind my bones and I can tell by Veil's posture he's losing patience with us.

I halt the group and sigh. "*What* are you doing?"

"What's the matter?" asks Donar. "Keep moving or we'll freeze to death."

"Is there something up my ass of interest to you?"

"Eden, you're being unreasonable," says Elvandra. "You're a loner, we get it, but we're all cold and scared and we can only see as far as your torch. The closer we stay the safer we'll be. If you don't like it, give Veil the flame."

I laugh. "You think The Hood won't smack one of you for getting too close any less than I will? Stay close, yes. Touch me, no. *Got it*?"

Elvandra nods and Donar holds up both arms, sighing. They're frustrated with me but it's for their own good. If we're attacked I'll be aiming at the closest moving target, be it a friend or foe because out here, I'll have no idea who's who. Any of these people could turn a weapon on me, desperate for extra rations or clothing when the journey gets tough. I'm not giving them the opportunity to be mistaken for my enemy either, or I for theirs.

I thrust the torch forward and watch my step, careful not to get caught in fallen vines, ditches or step on anything venomous. When I'm a good few paces ahead I pause and the group halt behind me.

"*Dante.*"

I shove aside any branches and shrubbery in my way. There, half-hidden beneath the snow and dirt, is my copy of Dante's work, given to Warden in my cell during our last intimate conversation.

"Warden passed through here," I say, my lip quivering. "He's *alive*."

"We don't know that," says Amani

I sink to my knees and cradle the battered book, now missing several pages. The remaining sheets are stuck together and the colours of the pictures have smudged. Still, I slide it into my bag and struggle to my feet, leaning against a tree for support.

"There are no tracks," I hear Veil say. "If he passed through here, snow has fallen since."

"There's no other way out," says Elvandra. "He *definitely* passed through here."

Donar points ahead, drawing our attention to some broken branches. "Left a less obvious trail."

"We should follow," says Chastity. "It's safest with Warden."

I clench my fists. "We're not in prison any longer, Four. Warden only cares for Warden unless there's something he wants that's worth your company." I swallow hard and turn away, careful not to let the kid see me cry. "Do you think out here he's interested in what's beneath your skirt?"

Chastity's face reddens. "He never-"

"Save it," says Veil. "Eden, I agree with Four. Warden survived so far; if he is injured we may be able to find him. Safety in numbers. That is what we decided, however stupid."

I hand over the torch and let Veil lead the way.

"You're not walking with Veil?" asks Chastity. "What if something creeps up on you? How can you outrun it?"

I narrow my eyes and shove the kid aside. "I don't need to outrun the monster, I just need to outrun *you*."

"Corrina was right about you," she whimpers.

"Oi, you two! Pack it in," Rae orders. "Every hungry beast within ten miles will hear your bickering."

"I assure you, Eden, you may be able to outrun

Chastity but nobody outruns The Hood." Veil grins. "If you die, I get some peace and quiet."

"You're funny, Veil. Perhaps whilst you entertain them with your jokes, *we* can gain a head start."

It's relatively quiet the farther from Titan we walk. In the distance there's a warm glow emanating from the horizon. The ark must be on fire, drawing the animals and banished inmates toward it like a dinner bell. Those not trapped or dead are in for a fight so I'm pleased we got away. The forest isn't an ideal home for a species so accustomed to artificial light and rationed porridge, but the sense of freedom is intoxicating.

We trek for another three hours and at least seven or eight miles before coming to some ruins; the base of a building which has been overgrown with weeds and its windows smashed. I can't understand how six hundred years ago, humans were motivated enough to build such beautiful structures, towering high and powerful. After the apocalypse, it would have made more sense to build thick, tall and impenetrable buildings to keep out predators, radiation and warlords, but by the time humanity realised how badly they needed such sense, it was too late.

"Eden," Veil calls, "there is blood here."

I skip past the others and slip to a halt in the snow, almost dropping my bag. Veil's right, there's blood. A lot of it and fresh, too. The sticky crimson is everywhere; sprayed across leaves, leaving pretty patterns in the snow and then disappearing in thick drag marks through the trees and into darkness. The blood begins first, suggesting a head wound. Whoever fell here was dragged by their feet. If they didn't die instantly as I'd hope out of mercy, they bled out not far from us.

The inmate in me wants to investigate and seek Warden's body. She's got no doubt it's him. The civilian in me wants to haul ass in the opposite direction. She's too filled with self-preservation to give a damn who's at the end of the trail.

"Oh, this is bad," says Ginny. "Not sure I've got this in me. I'm no hardcore survivor, Veil. Can't we just build a shelter and sit this out until daylight?"

"Finally you've got something to say and it's completely useless," I growl. "Logic says to follow the trail."

"I'm sorry, don't you want to live?" he snaps.

Veil rolls his eyes. He kneels silently, scoops up some snow and pelts the back of Ginny's head with it. He caught a splodge of blood which stains the collar of his coat, then aims his next missile at me.

Ginny scoops the ice from his neck and flicks it back. "How are you *not* scared?" he says. "There is blood trickling down my back. Do you see this?"

His voice increases in volume the more he moves and his arms begin to flail.

"I see it but I am undisturbed by it."

"Are you *twisted*? I can't take this anymore. Come on Rachana, we're leaving." Ginny rubs his eyes and makes a quick decision, then storms away from the blood. "Heading this way."

"Not cool, Veil," I say, stifling a chuckle. "What was the point?"

"That man is far too tense; he will get us all killed if he does not loosen up."

I shrug, but Chastity only frowns and shakes her

head. "He just lost his brother," she says. "A little empathy, maybe?"

Rae grunts. "We've all lost somebody to Titan."

Veil begins to walk after Ginny, figuring even though the fool is endangering us all with his rash decisions, we can still offer him a small amount of protection.

"Veil, wait." Chastity chases after him. "You're making a mistake. We shouldn't be following, we should be convincing him to find Warden."

I catch her twice and almost have to a third when her slick shoes send her skidding across a clearing. Veil spins when the wind catches his hood. The sight of his scarred skin clearly startles the blonde because she pins her body against the nearest tree and outstretches her hands.

"Look, kid," I tell her, "Veil only got this far for being Veil. Sure, he's arrogant and selfish, self-contained and anti-social." I pause and glance at Veil whose arms are now tightly folded. His eyes narrow, waiting for the end of my statement. "He's alive because he's capable of separating his memories and experiences from current happenings; doesn't take everything so personal and storm off without thinking whenever he's angry. Ginny lost face for a few moments and he's embarrassed because he's Rachana's guardian, for now."

Chastity nods but her eyes have already glazed. Her mind is beyond the trees already, wondering what else is lurking. Veil snaps his fingers and regains her attention. She backs so hard against that tree, I imagine her climbing it.

"We should all harden our hearts."

"To the people we love?" she asks, releasing the pressure a little. She blinks the falling snow off her lashes and cradles her chilled shoulders. "Not that I have family left; they're likely all dead or running." Chastity pauses, "Doesn't Elvandra have a sister?"

"Flona," I reply. "If she's anything like Rae she'll be dead already."

"How can you say such things? Elvandra is a lovely-"

"Yes, there's no doubt. Elvandra didn't run after Flona because there is little point. It may seem cruel to some but to others it is logical."

Watching my footing I head toward Ginny's trail and ignore the girl, hoping she'll close her mouth and follow rather than challenging our every decision. When we catch up, Ginny is a statue in the middle of a blank sheet of snow. There are footsteps leading out and Rachana watches from the branch of a fallen tree.

"Why have we stopped?"

Veil sets off across the clearing and is met by a piercing scream of warning. Rachana hops from her tree and points at Ginny's posture. Rae holds her back.

"It's ice. Don't move, it'll break!"

I cringe at the volume of her threat and scan our surroundings. Sure enough, she's drawn the attention of some mutants whose feet can be heard thundering our way in the distance. I touch my finger to my lips and point up, gesturing for everyone to take to the trees and hide. Everyone but Ginny, of course, whom Veil and I will now have to save.

"What now?" I whisper when everyone is out of sight.

Aeon Infinitum: Run For Your Life

The footsteps become heavier and the added sound of snapping branches sends shudders down my spine. Any minute now, we're dead. Ginny's patch of ice doesn't appear too wide but it's long like a stream, leading me to presume it's not too deep. If he was to break through, Veil and I are fast and strong enough to haul him up before he's sucked under completely. Worst case scenario, Veil will have to hold off the creatures until I can smash another hole and pull Ginny out by his collar.

Ginny turns gently on his shoes and I can see his eyes are filled with tears. Then I realise, even if we did manage to pull him free, within a few hours he'd be dead from hypothermia anyway. Wet clothing in this weather can only add to the pain of frost-bitten limbs. Unless a member of our group donates something at their own expense or if Wardrobe rustles up an emergency outfit, he'll perish.

"Come back the way you came. Follow your footsteps," Veil orders.

From the corner of my eye I spot movement and the creature is on me before I can draw my weapon. It's a humanoid but its nose and jaw are extended like that of a bear and hair reaches down its entire back. Instead of nails there are claws, curved and needle-sharp. They dig through my layers of clothing and tear holes in them, letting in a draught so cold I can imagine the skin beneath turning blue. I writhe and yell at Veil to get Ginny to safety but he's out of time. A second beast lunges from the foliage and knocks Ginny on his back, breaking the ice and sending them both underwater. Ginny emerges a few seconds later. Blood covers his face turning the water crimson. He swallows so much water I think he'll drown before the animal can maul him to death, which is probably kinder. Veil has drawn his weapon and is, without mercy, hacking at the thing that's pinning me to the snow. It's heavy, overweight and the stench of wet dog is excruciatingly poignant.

I notice through the panic that this creature doesn't bare the unusual glow of those back at the silo. This thing is one hundred percent wild and rabid.

"Veil!"

I throw my arms out at him to bat him away.

The creature's jaw widens and from it crawls a thick pink tongue. It meets my face, caressing the sweat, blood and filth from the forest and then its teeth become vibrant in the moonlight. They're heading for my shoulder and I'm completely helpless. Even Veil's sword can't penetrate its thick skin and its back leg defends Veil's brutal attempts at murder.

I cry out when a chunk of flesh from my shoulder is torn away, leaving a bloody mess of meat and fabric. The beast chews slowly, taking care to taste and swallow every inch of its food in case the next isn't quite so easy to catch. The pain is harrowing and my consciousness is beginning to fade when I catch sight of Ginny re-emerging, beast free.

Veil follows my line of sight.

"Go," I gasp. "Go now!"

And with my final order, he's gone.

15

Ginny Bede

Snarls, gurgles and screams fill the clearing as Veil beheads Eden's monster. Between each mouthful of river water, splatter of blood and shout from the trees above us, I hear Eden telling Veil to leave; to let her die. Her shoulder is mauled and she's bleeding out. The snow surrounding her body is vibrant and melting from escaping heat.

"Veil! Help Eden."

Veil stops between us, looks back over his shoulder and shakes his head.

"She is a lost cause."

"Don't, I drowned it," I tell him. "It panicked and dragged me under. The ice trapped it down there." I point at a patch of broken ice through the trees and from it a wet paw hangs loose. "Huge and hairy but not so smart. See to Eden," I say and wave him away.

Rachana jumps down from her tree and carefully creeps across the ice to help me out of the water.

"No you'll fall too and we haven't enough clothing to change both of us. Those scraps of tree over there, fetch them."

Rachana nods and grabs as many thick branches as

she can, then lays them to create a path. I haul my body onto them and then slide my weight evenly across until I hit dry land. Already I feel the chill of the weather through my soaked clothing and Rachana is rooting furiously through her bag to find me some replacement pants and a thick jumper. Elvandra hands me a scarf and sacrifices her socks, given that the only spare shoes are thin and unlikely to keep out the cold. With effort from everyone, I'm soon dressed, albeit randomly, in warm clothing.

"That is why we keep our voices *down*," Veil growls.

"She didn't mean to cause trouble, Veil," Rae reasons.

Veil snatches Rachana's bag and pulls out as many of the medical supplies as we can realistically spare, then drops beside Eden. She's unconscious which is for the best and her arm is coated in a slick red paste of blood, dirt and mutant saliva. When Veil shakes her and taps her face, she groans but her eyes never open.

"Stupid girl," he grumbles. "Ginny, control your brat next time."

"Hardly *my* fault," I say, burying my wet clothing to hide the scent of human.

"No?" Donar finally plucks up some courage. "If you hadn't taken this route and ignored the trail of blood back there, we wouldn't have hit the ravine in the first place."

Elvandra wraps Donar in an embrace. "We're all exhausted and scared. Perhaps we should find somewhere to hide for a couple of hours. Veil and I can dress Eden's wound. Chastity, grab my bag; there should be some antibiotics in there somewhere."

"We have medication?" she asks, eyes wide.

"Stolen from the infirmary," Elvandra replies. "On any other occasion people like us, of our class, would be left to die. Flona used to deal in pharmaceuticals before she became, well, you know."

"Why would you go from being a chemist to a prostitute?" Amani asks.

Elvandra scowls. "She knew too much, but nothing she could prove so instead of killing her they demoted her, all right? Now let it go. Thanks to my sister Eden is probably going to survive, but who can tell what's going to fester in that wound."

"That's what the antibiotics are for," Donar says.

"The world's moved on a lot since they were last tested outside Titan." Elvandra sighs. "For all we know she could wake a mutant."

"One of those monstrosities?" Amani shakes his head.

"She will not thank me if I let her turn," Veil adds.

"She's not going to eat you, but she may lose her arm and whatever diseases that creature was carrying when it chewed a hole in her will have been transferred. Our petty human pills might not fight such illnesses. Now come on, we have to move her," Rae says.

Eden groans when Veil lifts her by the shoulders and I grab her legs. Even with Veil's help, she's heavy and although I never thought it possible, more stubborn when unconscious. We carry her for a mile or so before my own arms are beginning to ache and Donar starts mumbling something about his growling stomach.

"We can't stay in the open." Elvandra, for the first

time since leaving Titan, rests her designs on the snow and reaches into her pack. "Here, take the bread and fruit and find somewhere to hide. Don't light a fire, you'll give our position away. Donar and I will go hunting."

Veil snorts. "*You* want to hunt?"

"Yes Veil, I want to hunt. You and Ginny have been carrying the inmate, so it's only fair we play our part. Without Corrina and Juliette to help, who else is there?"

"How about me and Amani?" asks Chastity.

Rae smiles. "You should stay and take care of Eden. Here, let me show you how to bandage the wound before I go."

Veil grips my arm and drags me aside, then lowers his hood. His scars look even more brutal and intimidating in the darkness; it's like he belongs out here, or that the mutants claimed him. I remind myself that Veil was bitten and still bears the markings of the hunter's teeth but pulled through without infection or mutation, at least to my knowledge.

"Ginny, we are being watched," he says, keeping his eyes lowered and our bodies close, which for Veil is uncomfortable. I can tell. "Just beyond those trees, hunkered low."

"Should we do something?" I whisper, managing to control my curiosity.

If we draw attention to them, they'll either run or fight. I'd rather they didn't jump out with weapons; with one of our best warriors in a critical condition, two of our smartest minds out hunting and only a hooded teen and innocent children to back me up, our odds of victory are slim to none.

Veil shakes his head. "Act natural."

"What a *stupid* thing to say," I tell him, rolling my eyes. "Nothing about this is natural."

His grip tightens. "I am not suggesting you bend over and graze. Make yourself useful. In the meantime, I am going to find and use Eden's bow. I saw her with it back at Titan."

"Are you sure because I haven't seen any arrows. She'll kick your ass if she catches you in her bag," I say.

There's a light rustle in the leaves as whoever our unwanted guest is decides to switch positions or head back to their own camp. It may be another escapee, a less dangerous mutant or nobody at all. Veil could simply be worrying over a passing animal, but his experience in the wilderness leads me to believe him more than my gut.

Rachana is close by my side and hears most of the conversation but decides it is best not to comment. Veil is already angry with her for drawing the mutants' attention to our whereabouts, for almost getting Eden and I eaten alive and for generally being in his way. She tugs my sleeve when Veil wanders into the darkness, blending perfectly, without saying goodbye.

"Is Veil coming back?"

I nod. "He's dealing with a nearby pest."

"Oh." She smiles and kneels beside Eden. "I might need your help, Ginny. Elvandra talked us through the basics but the wound is still bleeding. Do you think she'll lose the arm?"

"Amputation isn't on my list of skills, kid."

"Mine neither," Chastity says.

"Here, put pressure on this part for me. I have to wrap up the bite."

I do as I'm instructed and press hard before the open wound to prevent the flow of blood whilst Rachana wraps it in a soft white bandage. We're out of tape and safety pins. These were always a luxury so, for now, we'll have to do with a tight knot and frequent fabric changes.

Eden is still asleep when the whoosh of an arrow flies over our heads and hits a tree thirty yards away. Whoever was watching us takes off into the trees, sprinting too fast for any of us to catch up.

Veil re-emerges. "I made some arrows. Did you see where he went?" I shake my head. "Then we should go now before he returns."

"No. Elvandra and Donar are still out there; we can't leave them," Chastity says. "Please, Veil. Let us wait for them. Eden isn't well enough."

"Chastity's right," Amani says. "We can't move her yet. I need to try to get her to swallow these antibiotics."

Veil ignores our protests and gathers his things, then follows the mystery guest into the depths of the forest, leaving us alone and unprotected. I reach into my pack and retrieve a knife but it's not sharp or long enough to do any real damage.

My mind skates back to the mutant that attacked Eden and how Veil, the strongest and most experienced of our group, hacked at the beast's armour with his sword. Nothing happened. A few dents and bruises, maybe, but only when he aimed at the head did he do any real damage and it would have been equally as easy to miss and decapitate Eden instead.

"Do you think he'll find them?" Amani asks.

"No," I reply, "and we shouldn't worry about such a

danger until it's upon us. Right?"

"Right," Rachana says, then sits Eden up and rests her head against my pack.

Her skin blends with the snow and even though her eyelids twitch and she grumbles occasionally, I begin to doubt if she'll pull through. I hope she will.

Eden is a fighter; always has been, even before she met Warden.

Warden and I were friends for years before he and Eden found one another and by then it was too late to stop their plans to assassinate Czar. Of course, I agreed he deserved the fate but staring at her blank expression it's difficult to agree her actions didn't, in part, lead us to where we are today. If it weren't for their stupidity, Czar might never have doubted the integrity of his citizens and therefore decided, less than a year later, to activate the Harmony Grid.

I lean over and kiss Eden's forehead but her eyes startle open before I can withdraw my lips.

"Eden, I'm sorry I scared you. How are you fe-"

Her arm raises, pointing at something in the distance. Rachana, Chastity and I turn in unison to be faced by a man three times my size; his muscles are thick and his face covered with black hair. He approaches on the balls of his feet with his hands raised. What I think is a smile is painted upon thin lips which are purple from the cold, but despite the signs he's freezing, he wears little clothing.

"Come," he says and gestures. "Come."

Eden isn't strong enough to stand. Amani and Chastity are now cowering behind me.

"No." I shake my head. If he can't understand our

language, perhaps he'll understand the gesture. "My friend, she's sick."

I point at Eden and make a claw with my hand, then fake an attack.

"Bitten?" asks the man, crouching low and resting on his knuckles like an ape. "Soon?"

"I don't under-"

"He wants to know when she was bitten," says Rachana. She turns to the man and offers him the bottle of pills. "Soon." She smiles. "We need help."

"Come," he repeats and then disappears beyond the tree line.

Rachana and I struggle to help Eden to her feet. Without being asked, Chastity takes hold of her bag and helps fasten mine to my back, then we're on our way. Veil, having taken off alone and without protection, is now either dead or lost in the labyrinth of woodland and ruins with nothing to use as a guide. He didn't take our map so he could be anywhere.

We trudge behind the unnamed man, hopeful he can cure our friend.

16

Elvandra Rae

The darkness has killed so much, I can hardly bear it.

As a child, Flona and I often visited the library, reading stories about the world as it once was before NORA. Before the tsunamis, earthquakes, volcanic eruptions and seemingly endless nights, the world was a wonderful but sensitive place. Life thrived in every corner, adapting to its habitat and evolving gracefully. Humans were advanced in technology and fashion, intelligent and emotionally whole. Their music inspired. Their books filled the hearts and souls of readers and work was as valued for social interaction as for making money.

Structures spanned the horizon; high-rise buildings towered above the tiny creatures moving below, dodging the traffic of mechanical transportation. Light from cities acted as beacons for alien worlds, seen far from space and as the world moved on, so did time. I used to think it sounded like a fascinating, almost fantastical place to exist with open opportunities and freedom around every corner.

Now, as I creep on my toes with my blade raised at

shoulder height behind Donar, I struggle to feel anything for the remnants of the old earth other than frustration. The ruins give every harmless and edible living thing on *Ad Infinitum* a place to hide, be it an old sewer or train station, a crumbled office block, the overgrown grounds of a school or even a prison. Beneath my feet still glistens shattered glass, entwined barbed wire and broken pots. It's impossible to be invisible when everything around us only highlights our presence.

"This is impossible. Let's go back," I tell Donar, tugging on his shoulder. He shakes his head and gestures for me to be quiet whilst ducking behind a collapsed wall. "What is it?"

Donar points north toward the remains of a road and grazing there is a deer. From here I think it's like those I've seen in pictures. Completely normal, unlike the mutated, strange creatures the Ventures showed us in training. My mind skates to Eden's injury and I know we need this kill if she's to build up her strength and survive. More to the point, if she's to guide us all to safety with her.

"On my count," he whispers, but I'm too eager.

I pounce from behind the wall and throw the blade handle first at the deer. It goes spinning through the air, creating a whooshing noise and a thunk as it misses and strikes a tree.

Donar sighs and steps into the clearing, then aims his knife and releases before the deer can escape. It strikes clean and humanely. With barely a whimper, the deer is dead and ours for the taking. Together we kneel and assess the weight of the animal against the distance we're supposed to carry it.

I retrieve my knife.

"Elvandra, *what* was that?"

"A deer. We killed it."

Donar rolls his eyes. "You know what I mean; why did you dash out?"

"Excitement," I say, forcing eye contact. "Eden needed food and the longer we left it, the more likely another predator would beat us to this feast. Sorry."

Donar shrugs. "Fine, but think next time. You might have scared it off. I haven't seen any other *normal* animals around here since we escaped Titan."

"Perhaps we're being cared for," I say, smiling. "Or the world is beginning to heal?"

"I doubt anyone cares more about my life than I do right now. Come on, let's haul this thing back to camp. If Eden's awake she'll be creating a scene. Do you still have the drugs we stole from Titan's infirmary?"

"Some," I reply, "but the antibiotics are in short supply and she'll use them quickly. If we can, we should find some natural remedies on our way back. How are you at biology?"

"Not so good," he says, "but I think the inmates studied this in their training for a few hours. Perhaps Chastity and Amani will recognise something if we take back a selection of shrubs."

Donar grabs the hind legs and I take the head, then together we drag the deer through the snow and back toward the others. We're almost back when Veil appears from the darkness with his hood lowered. He's out of breath and red-faced.

"What do we have here?" he asks, forcing a smile. "You saved me the job. A deer. You did well."

"Oh, so you *do* show gratitude." Donar dumps the back end of the deer and wipes his forehead.

"When it suits me. Is this our lunch?"

"We're willing to share but Eden needs this more than us, Veil. She's weaker than we are."

"True; given she is our best chance at survival other than yours truly, I can promise her first bite."

Veil takes over at my end, but I'm not convinced he's here to help.

"Where are the others, Veil?" I ask with folded arms. "You didn't leave them alone?"

"Ginny is with them. I thought I would explore the area." He never blinks. "Satisfied?"

"No, actually," Donar says. "Aren't you terrified of the outer world, considering what happened to you last time? So what's *really* going on Veil. We can handle it."

Cooling off, Veil decides to replace his hood. Partly to keep the draught off his neck and hide his body language from Donar and I. Something is wrong because stern-faced teenagers don't bolt into the unknown for nothing, leaving behind their only source of company and safety.

"I thought we were being watched. I heard noises."

"Seems likely. We're in the wild," I reply.

"We are being followed. More reason to move this feast before whomever they are decide to challenge us for it." Veil pauses and shakes his head. "Never thought I would have to prepare myself mentally and fight over the carcass of a deer."

"Food is worth fighting for," I remind him. "So do you have any idea who they are?"

"Warden, maybe," he replies. "Though Eden cannot

hear about my suspicions until they are confirmed. Our vicious little inmate is in no condition to be chasing ghosts across *Ad Infinitum*. Still, Warden is, beneath the surface, a coward. Cowards rely on others to do their bidding and hide behind the decisions of others. He is Czar's most trusted guard, protected by his title and the power it supplies. My vote is on Warden."

"He's not stupid enough to challenge us for the meal," Donar says. "That could end only in death or serious injury. Eden wouldn't trust him again. In fact, the way she's been behaving I wouldn't be shocked if she gutted him herself and strung him from the nearest tree."

"Donar! What a horrid thing to say," I scold.

"The truth hurts, sometimes," he replies. "Less talk, more work. Elvandra, see if you can find us some plants and berries for the inmates to have a look at. We might fall lucky this time."

"And if they're poison to touch?" I ask, my hands trembling from the cold.

Veil's eyes narrow. "Then we will miss you."

I'm still grumbling about Veil's hideous sense of humour when we reach the camp, but at the sight of an empty clearing and confused footprints, the air leaves my lungs. I'm panicking. Where are they? What's happened to them?

"Veil! Donar! Quick!"

Veil skids to a halt in the snow beside me and curses beneath his breath. He examines the prints and the drag mark, indicating that Rachana, Ginny, Amani and Chastity dragged an unconscious Eden to safety, but who do the other set of prints belong to?

"Somebody else was here," Veil says. "Warden,

perhaps."

"We don't know that," says Donar, dropping his end of the deer. "Why would he trick them?"

"I do not trust him," Veil says.

"I didn't trust you but now we're the *best* of friends."

Veil scolds me with a stern growl and a tightened fist, but I ignore his malfunctioning manners.

"Warden and Eden were in love once, right?"

Donar nods, although none of us fully understand what happened between them.

"Those feelings can't simply melt away," I continue. "If Warden's alive and they stumble upon one another, they're going to stick together. The more of us the better. Perhaps we should have reinforced that rule before we lost the others."

"It was nobody's fault that Eighteen died but her own," Veil says. His voice becomes flat and emotionless. "People die, we move on. I do not plan to perish out here, especially crying over those who were not strong enough."

"Corrina's strength wasn't the issue," I remind him. "In my opinion, the terrifying mutant dog thing was the cause of death, *not* her courage."

"Strength and courage are separate," Donar argues. "Corrina was both strong and courageous, but her heart wasn't in this journey."

"What gave you the impression that *mine* was?" I ask.

"Elvandra, don't you know she planned to hide Chastity and opt out of the banishment?" Donar says.

Veil tuts. "Impossible."

"Her references to the evil inside Eden weren't

because of her hardened shell or her inability to make friends, it was because of her reaction to Corrina's plan."

"You're saying that Eden told Corrina not to bother hiding the girl?"

"Of course," he says. "Eden saw early on how awful this would be."

I take my knife and, using the best of my knowledge from the library, begin carving up the meat. If it's in smaller proportions, split between the three of us, it'll be far easier to carry. Donar's kitchen experience will hopefully come in handy when we have to cook it.

Veil interjects. "A fast death, even if bloody and gruesome, is better than extended and painful. If I am to die before the sunrise, my plan is to go smoothly and as painlessly as possible. Why drag out the inevitable; have time to worry about what you cannot control? No," he says, shaking his head. "Eden was right to deny the success of that plan."

"There's no guarantee death is easier out here, though," Donar reasons. "Eden is a perfect example. That bite could kill her. She'll be in severe pain, perhaps unable to tell us just how bad it really is."

"Better to have a fifty-fifty chance though," I say.

"If it were up to me," says Veil, "and Eden was suffering any more than in her current state, I would be pleased to end her life. Do not argue with me, Elvandra. I know what you are going to say."

"I wasn't going to," I lie.

"Tell me, in Eden's position with your arm mauled to the bone, a possible mutation creeping through your veins with the likelihood that you will turn on those you love, what action would you want Donar to take?" Veil asks. "Be honest."

"He'd put me down early," I admit.

"I couldn't murder somebody who might recover though." Donar shudders. "We're not all like you, Veil."

I scowl at my Wardrobe colleague in disgust. What Veil did for Eden was as expected and as he was asked. Eden knew her chances of survival against Ginny's were slim and Veil took necessary actions to rescue who he believed would pull through. The person who could help the group take another step toward safety. Had he chosen Eden without Ginny's go ahead, they might *both* have perished and taken Veil with them.

"Donar, please, this isn't the time or place to pick fault with the one person who can keep us alive right now."

"We're more capable than you give us credit for. We'd be fine without him, Rae. I killed that deer without any trouble."

"Let's stop fighting and follow whoever took our friends. We'd want the same if we got captured, *right*?"

Donar nods. "Veil, perhaps you can get a head start whilst Elvandra and I finish carving up the portions. We'll catch up."

"Not after the last time. It is Ginny's fault Eden was attacked. His and that little mutant's," Veil says, angrily. His eyes narrow. "We will stay together."

"*What* mutant?" I ask, my brows furrowed in concern.

"I may be young but I am no fool, Elvandra. I heard you and the kid discussing her ability in the tower."

"You were eavesdropping?"

"It is hardly eavesdropping when you were three

feet from my bed."

"Veil, you're not considering killing her?" I panic.

Rachana trusted me with her secret; she's going to think I told the murderous teenager.

"If so then reconsider because I was thinking she may be able to transfer some of her, uhm, ability, and save Eden's arm."

"I may not like her company but I have nothing against her nature." Veil nods once and then disappears into the darkness, his voice growing darker, too. "Leave the rest of that deer for whoever is following. Perhaps if they feed they will leave us be."

Donar and I glance around. We collect our things quickly.

"We're still being followed?" I ask.

We wait in the silence of the lightly falling snow for a response, but receive none. I turn to Donar, concerned.

"Should we follow him?"

"There's enough meat here to feed us for a week. I say we abandon the rest."

"Then he'll gloat until our mysterious follower reappears, no doubt." I grin. "Donar, what do you think we're going to find at the end of this trail? I'm not sure I want to see pieces of my friends strewn across some ancient ruins or dangling from a tree."

He straps his pack around his shoulders and waist, then shrugs. "Veil wouldn't lead us toward danger. He's too clever; it's like he feels the warnings of this world all around him. In the air, in the water, in the shadows. *Ad Infinitum* talks to him."

I swallow hard. "And what do you suppose it's saying?"

After a few seconds, Donar smiles and pats me on the shoulder. "That it's bloody freezing and we ought to get a move on. Like it or not I think we're stuck with The Hood."

"Come on then. Let's get out of here."

Donar and I chase after Veil with a hefty bag of venison to feed our group and begin following his tracks in the snow. Without the sunlight and the dinner bells of Titan to tell us when to eat, we're going to be forced to listen to the growling in our stomachs and hope they synchronise.

If we continue walking at this pace, the first star on the map should be fast approaching. Who knows what we'll find when we arrive, if anything, or who might be waiting for us. For now, though, I pray that the predator on our trail appreciates our donation and treats it as the peace offering we were never fortunate enough to receive from Czar.

17

Eden Maas

It's a miracle I'm still breathing.

My arm is wrapped tightly in several shades of bandage and cloth, tied with the rope from Chastity's outfit. I feel guilty for taking it, even against my will, and force a smile at both Rachana and Chastity for their help. Chastity has a tin cup to my lips and Rachana has covered me with a blanket I don't recognise. Although a little damp from the weather, I'm warm and comfortable, but my stomach is growling.

"Where am I?"

My head is pounding like something has been knocked loose and is rattling around in my skull, taking extra care to smack the back of my eyeballs. It's nothing in comparison to the seething pain in my arm or the dizziness.

"What happened to me?"

"You were attacked by a rabid mutant," Amani says. "Our friend dragged you here and gave us some food."

I startle and throw back the blanket, preparing to flee. My bow is missing and I'm not strong enough to run, but this stranger is tall and broad; clumsy looking and could potentially be slow, even slower than an injured inmate.

"Who are you?"

"Fox," he says, tapping his chest. He crouches beside me, examining my shoulder and reaches out to touch the bandage. I pull away, but he's persistent. "Fox. Eden," he says, smiling.

"I'm officially freaked out. What *is* this thing?"

"He's Fox," says Ginny, entering through a door I hadn't even noticed.

The whole room is full of them. There are four doors in all directions of the compass and my curiosity is drawn to them all.

"Don't worry, he's a friend. He helped save us. With Elvandra and Donar out hunting and Veil chasing a shadow, we were beginning to feel abandoned. He appeared and pointed us here. I've checked the map, Eden, this is one of the sanctuaries, though we haven't made it fifty miles. It's strange if you ask me."

"Have others passed through?" I ask Fox, then remember he doesn't speak our tongue. "Uhm, how do I say others?" I hesitate and point to my friends. "More people?"

Fox raises an eyebrow. *This isn't working.*

"Ginny? Anyone else here, as far as you know?"

"No, just Fox. Though he comes and goes. I think this is a storage facility of some kind and he's a messenger. He takes things and goes out, then returns a few hours later with something else."

"He's a tradesman?"

"Not necessarily," says Rachana. "He could be a runner. Perhaps it's his job, navigating the outside world. If there are others like us, more Titans I mean, maybe they found him and use him. If he's lived alone in the wilderness for a long time, I'll bet he knows which routes are safest. If you ask me, we should follow him."

"What about the others?" I ask. "Rae, Donar and Veil?"

"I'm sorry, Eden, but we had to get you somewhere warm and dry. You were bleeding out. Fox stitched the wound and gave us these pills. They've worked much faster than I thought they would but the label says may cause drowsiness and dizziness." Ginny forces a smile and insists I drink more water. "Rachana took one first to be sure they weren't dangerous."

"I heal quickly," she replies.

"Thank you, I think. How do *you* feel?"

"Great," she says, beaming. "My vision is clearer and my muscles are less achy. Still, my body fights infection faster than most people, so I've noticed. The effects won't last long. On you, I have no doubt they'll help your recovery."

I'm still not convinced whether I'm dreaming or truly awake. Between the kid's babbling, Ginny's constant awkward smiles and Fox's curious pokes and prods, I'm not focused or ready to deal with new problems yet. If only I could drift back to sleep and awake in my own bed, or even in my cell. I'd take foot rot any day over this nightmare.

"We should find our friends," I tell Fox. "Uhm, friends. Out there." I point at the door, but Fox just grunts and takes the cup from me. "This is, *unbelievable*. Is he an ape or a human or, a mutant?"

"I think evolution chose a new path," said Chastity. Her voice is minute against the booming of Rachana's confident tongue. "It's reversed. Like the world realised humans were destructive and evolution wasn't going to make the same mistake again, so it threw progress into reverse."

"In just six hundred years?"

"It's amazing, isn't it?" Ginny says. "I couldn't believe it either. Before NORA hit and threw everything off balance, humans were doing a good job of destroying nature anyway. Perhaps there are gods watching over us who decided we didn't deserve to progress and instead, whilst we've been hibernating below the surface in Titan, they'd figure out a way to finish us off."

"I don't believe in god. So there are no more humans as we know them?" I ask, fearful Ginny may be right.

"Interesting idea, isn't it?"

"No, I hate it."

Ginny holds out a hand and aids me to a wobbly stance. A few steps and I'm exhausted, but it feels good to be at my regular height again, surveying my surroundings from over five feet rather than two.

The room is plain and cool, but it's weatherproof because in here there is no breeze, no snow and no rain. The walls are brick but the doors are wooden, and there's an old shaggy rug on the floor. The contents are minimal too, but as Ginny said there's no doubt it's a storage facility. There are signs above the doors, directing Fox to the goods he's holding and there isn't much furniture around.

"Traveller's symbols?" I ask, pointing to the first one I spot. "There were people here like us."

"It's a universal language, Eden," Ginny reasons. "Fox draws pictures a lot like a caveman. He uses charred wood to scratch black outlines onto the brick. See this one here?"

He guides me to a picture of a stick man with a circle around his head, like a bowl or a *hood*.

"That's Veil. He's seen Veil?" I stagger toward Fox and point at the drawing. "Can you show me him?" I lead Fox to the wall and tap it. "Do you know where he is?"

Fox nods and hoots. He's seen my friends. They're alive.

"How about the house?" I ask.

Ginny smiles. "It means well-guarded house. On the way in here, it's painted on the door in red."

It's clear he's equally as excited as I am but I try not to raise my hopes. The symbol could have been painted by a humanoid like Fox. Holding a complete, interesting and informative conversation with him is beyond a challenge. Although, Fox knows what nodding your head means, pointing, smiling and other basic body language.

"Do you think Fox can lead us to Veil?" I ask, enthused.

"He'll do one better; I think he'll find him for us."

"Is there anyone more capable of keeping us breathing than The Hood?" Rachana asks. "I still don't like him. He's creepy."

Ginny nods. "The people Fox works for, maybe."

I don't like it. As much as I'd love a nice warm bath and some decent food, painkillers for my wound, fresh clothes and a roof over my head, we can't be sure Fox's people will welcome us. I'd like to think they'd be as overwhelmed with joy as Titan's inhabitants to learn *Ad*

Infinitum isn't completely dead and that other normal humans still exist, but wars wage over territory between the banished and the mutants. What's to say they won't immediately presume we mean them harm and shoot us on sight?

"Oh, I'm not sure you've thought this through," I admit. "What if Fox's friends are human and they deem our presence on Earth– which I presume they still call this godforsaken planet– a danger to their civilisation and try to eliminate the threat? The alternative would be more like Fox here, and so far we're not doing so well at communicating our needs. How can we explain Czar to this ape?"

Fox hoots and smiles, recognising his name and points once more to the drawing of Veil. I nod and smile back, although I'm sure it looks forced because the pain in my arm bites deep and hard. If we're to escape Fox's company we'll have to move quickly. I know my adrenaline won't last much longer.

"He's done nothing but help, Eden. Those pills he gave us worked miracles and he's been offering us food and clothing since we got here," Ginny says. "I don't think we need to fear him."

"How can you be sure? He doesn't speak!"

I gesture at the half human, half ape and whilst trying to keep the peace, tell Ginny exactly what I expect will happen to us if we pitch up alongside Fox at his community. It's a long, awkward story, based mostly upon the stories of war and disputes over land I've read about in the books our library held.

When I'm done, Ginny asks for my honest opinion of the outcome.

I reply, "Death."

"We can't mosey by without at least checking it out," Amani says, nudging Chastity. "What do *you* think?"

She shudders and tries to make herself smaller by wrapping her arms around her body and crouching in the corner. I see fear in her ocean eyes and whenever Fox moves, she does too, only away from him. Aloud she may not agree with my conclusion but inside she's screaming that I'm right.

"Don't know," she mumbles. "It's cold and I'm hungry. Can we stay here for a while longer?"

"Until we find the others it's unwise to move on," I tell her. "For now let's be thankful Fox isn't trying to eat us. On any other occasion– one when I'm preferably conscious– we wouldn't have landed in such a situation. Now we're here let's make the most of it."

I curl up under the blanket and cradle my arm. It's beginning to throb. Ginny thrusts another pill at me and insists I drink another cup of water.

"I can't keep my eyes open," I say. "Ginny, if I fall asleep, promise you'll try to convey to Fox that he needs to find Veil and bring him here. With any luck, he's already rounded up Donar and Elvandra."

"That I can do," he says, smiling. "Get some sleep. I'll wake you if anything happens."

I nod, then realise I should also warn him I may not wake up at all.

"Ginny, listen. If I don't rouse when you shake me or I lose more blood, forget about me, all right? You guys move on and lock this door behind you. I'll slow you down if my recovery time doesn't increase. Just make sure nothing can sniff me out."

Ginny places a gentle hand on my head. "I promise, but it won't come to that."

18

Ginny Bede

Eden's lashes flutter when her dreams cause a stir.

Occasionally she groans in agony and we cringe, praying the steady rise and fall of her chest continues. Rachana has checked her wound several times since we spoke and confirms there's no infection as far as she can see, which relaxes all of us. Eden is important to this journey; she's strong and motivated, persistent and hard-hearted when it's required. Without her, we're just cowards following a mentally challenged adolescent.

"Eden," Fox says, pointing at our sleeping friend. "Sick?"

"Yes, very sick." I hold up the bottle of pills and shake them. "Thank you."

Fox grins, balls his fists and smacks his chest. I sigh; maybe Eden is right. Fox is far less human that we'd first assumed and if he's being governed by a higher species, they won't appreciate filthy refuge seekers asking for aid on their doorstep. If Eden imagines their leader to be Czar's equivalent, we'd be in immediate danger.

Fox seems to be- although a happy one- their slave. So it's up to us to decide whether we'd like to risk being in the same situation or continuing, ignorant, to a possible Harmony Grid sanctuary.

Still, it concerns me this place is on the map but nobody else has attempted to reach the building and been rescued like we have. It terrifies me how easily Fox located us and how eager to help he was; surely if he's a slave he's under orders to do so and if not, he's intelligent enough not to act against their wishes, which would lead to punishment.

All these things circle in my mind when Fox jumps up and leaves without saying another word. Chastity and Rachana are startled and crawl toward me. He leaves through his usual door, ignoring the other three as he has since we arrived. If we are to discover the truth, we should investigate what lies behind the others.

Rachana takes one and Chastity, reluctant to move, takes another. I take the third and on the count of three we each push forward. Amani stays beside Eden in case she stops breathing.

Chastity's door is locked and I see from the way her muscles relax how pleased she is not to be moving through an unknown space into a possible trap, alone. Rachana's opens into a store cupboard. Fox must be fetching supplies from here when we're sleeping because I've never seen where he produces our food and clothing from. It's all canned and out of date, but it's food nevertheless.

My door creaks on its hinges and swings open, but the room is dimly lit. In the centre is a table and spread across in neat paper files are documents marked SECRET. I swallow hard and prop open the door with a piece of wood.

"Girls, I think I found something."

Rachana's head is the first to appear around the door and she races passed to take hold of the folders. Her eyes skate the information and her face loses colour.

"What is it?"

I take the paperwork from her and re-read the first page several times before it finally sinks in. The first paragraph refers to a natural disaster and the dinosaurs. We've all been tutored to know that, just like humans and NORA, they were wiped from Earth via a collision. Then, it moves on to discuss

PROJECT TARE.

I discover further down the page it stands for 'The Alien Race and Earth'. At that, my mind and my pulse begin to race.

We need to wake Eden.

I grab my pack and stuff the paperwork inside, then thrust it at Chastity and tell her to guard those documents with her life, which she doesn't take well. Eden's eyes flick open at the noise and she groans before sitting up. I have hold of her hand and am yanking her to her feet before she's fully regained consciousness or remembered where she is and why she's here.

"You were right. We need to go. *Now!*"

Eden's eyes widen. She yawns. "What's going on? Is Veil here?"

"Veil's dead," I reply, which is what I truly believe.

If Fox has any sense, he's tracked and murdered the others and plans to march us to his people for a similar fate, who, according to the secret documents, may be from another planet. If I pause to explain this now, we may not have time to clear the area and take whatever provisions we can with us. That's if Eden believes the story.

I still don't believe it myself.

I point to the locked door and tell Rachana to break it down. She begins to kick it repeatedly and, eventually, the ancient hinges come loose. I tear my attention away from Eden to help Rachana remove it, then light a candle and hold it at arm's length to check out the contents.

What I find is enough to fuel our escape.

On a chair, facing the back wall, is a very familiar figure.

"Oh my God." I gasp. "*Warden?*"

Eden shoves me aside, finding a boost of energy from the memory of their love. She falls to her knees, hisses as the shock finds the muscles in her arm and then rests it on Warden's knee. He's gagged and bound behind the chair; his eyes are wide with fury and fear and there are bruises around his neck, like somebody has attempted to strangle him within the past few days.

"What *happened* to you?" Amani asks, helping to untie him.

Eden rips the gag from his mouth and discards it on the floor. Warden wets his lips and breathes deeply.

"Where is he?" he asks, ignoring the worry in Eden's voice. "Is he gone?"

"Who?"

"The ape-man," Warden replies. "Quick, before he comes back, untie me!"

Rachana jolts forward, shoving Amani out of the way and fumbles with his restraints, trying to free his arms. Warden then unties his legs from the base of the chair which is bolted to the floor. Now it's a race to escape before Fox returns, but I'm unsure why.

"A couple of days ago, about twelve hours after Titan's collapse," he explains, "we were all running together. After I followed the Venturers to protest against leaving us, I heard the roof cave and thought I'd lost you all. Xander said not to bother trying to free you and that I should help him with the others, which I did against my will. Then the running started, and the fighting. I picked up some fallen citizens from the floor who were being trampled and then ushered them forward, moving toward the exit. When I fell though, nobody bothered to come back and help except for one. At first, I thought he looked like a banished inmate and tried to reason with him. He knocked me out and dragged me here. Ever since I've been locked in this room."

"Wait, you tried to come back for us?" Eden asks.

"Sure. I'm a monster and I'm selfish, but you and I have history, Eden, and my conscience couldn't live knowing I hadn't done everything I could to free you." Warden pauses. "And Chastity, I wanted to be sure she'd survived too."

"Of course you did," Eden sighs.

Rachana loosens the final knot and Warden is free, rubbing his aching wrists and heading for the exit, grabbing all he can on the way out. I'm unsure that theft from these people will help our case but leaving it behind for the taking won't help our survival either. Eden follows but I wait for the girls to leave before I dare.

"You're saying *Fox* did this to you? He's been so kind to us," I say.

Warden continues running until we're back out in the darkness, consumed by fear once more. Without a torch, I rely on the sounds of rustling footsteps and my friends' voices to navigate. Warden moves at a swift pace, eager to be away.

"He's sly," Warden replies, his breath laboured.

"This is insane," Rachana says. "Why save Eden's life if he wants to kill us?"

"He's not after you," Warden says. "He wants Veil. It seems our hooded recluse isn't quite as honest as he had you believe."

"*Meaning*?" I prompt.

Warden skids to a halt and turns so abruptly that Chastity crashes into the back of Rachana, knocking her down.

"Did *you* see the room too?" Amani asks.

"Yes, did you read the paperwork?"

I pick Rachana up by the elbow and frown. "Sure, I took the contents."

"Did you read it first?"

"Some," I admit. "Not all because I didn't have the chance."

Warden pinches his nose and snatches my bag, then produces a page I didn't have time to scan. He clears his throat.

"These pages speak of an 'owned adolescent'," he begins. "They describe Veil word-for-word; his mannerisms, his voice, his appearance and even his reaction to their experiments."

Chastity's minute voice quivers in the cold; a light white mist escapes her lips as she tries to cry, but can't summon the energy. Warden reaches out to take her hand but she pulls away, rightly trusting no-one.

Warden continues. "At first I thought they wrote this

to depict their findings and what they've observed of *Ad Infinitum*, or whatever they call it. But I was wrong. Fox let me out of the room only to eat and use the toilet, and sometimes he'd trust me not to attempt an escape. On those occasions I'd read a few lines more."

"Why not lock the door?" asks Rachana.

"I guess he never expected I'd escape or that you'd discover the truth." Warden shrugs. "It's irrelevant. Our government wrote this; these are copies of ancient documents that are over six hundred years old. When NORA hit, or what we *thought* was NORA, wiping out everything the planet knew, our government must have discovered what really arrived inside it and worked alongside them for a time. We studied one another. Veil, it appears, is their most recent test subject and he escaped."

"I don't understand," says Amani. "You mean, he was never banished?"

"Oh he was banished all right," Warden says, his brow raised. "He was just intercepted by them. He escaped and went through hell. That's why he doesn't remember anything."

Eden inhales sharply. I can't tell if it's shock or pain. "Veil knows where they are, whatever species we're talking about?"

Warden nods. "He's not the only one. Look."

He pulls out a double spread, marked with matching stars to Ginny's. It's a map of *Ad Infinitum* in black and white.

"Fox moves between these facilities, none of which are sanctuaries, I guarantee. The only one able to confirm what they really are, and what the purpose of the Harmony Grid really is, is Veil."

"Then we should find him," I say. "We think he might be with Donar and Elvandra. They went hunting and Fox found us before they returned. Veil set off on the trail of a lurker," he explains. "Said we were being watched."

"Perhaps the truth," Warden says. "Perhaps he knew his captors were back on his heels and he decided to end their hunt once and for all. He's vicious, merciless and experienced in the wilderness. Obviously, he recognised somebody and took off to speak with, or kill, that person."

"And how can we be sure this isn't just a story so you can manipulate us? Take our food and water and head off on your own across the grid; leave us to die or be mauled by a mutant. You and Fox may have drawn up this plan." Eden folds her arms as Warden dabs at the wounds on his face. "I'm not convinced Veil could be so heartless. He's young and has seen too much pain; pain a child should never witness, but I can't be sure he's such a brute unless I hear a confession direct from the accused."

"Then we find him," I repeat. "If Veil *is* guilty, we save Wardrobe from him and deal with the matter our own way. He's one boy against, well, *every* Titan survivor. If there are more of us, that is."

Warden hisses as he wipes blood from a split lip. "You don't get it. The excuse Czar gives about our prisons being full is nonsense. I may not be in on their secret, but I know for sure our prisons are far from full because Czar sends them all to their deaths out here. We haven't hung a prisoner in years."

"I don't understand," Eden says. "You killed the woman Corrina replaced. You killed Rachana's parents."

"No, we banished them. Actually, we fed them to these beasts. Did Veil say *anything* about what he saw when they opened the doors and released them?"

I cast my mind back to Veil's story about the beasts awaiting their lunch at Titan's boundary. The description he gave about how they paced, the way they looked, the crazed hunger in their eyes, their alien glow, and my heart drops to my stomach.

Warden grins. "He's lied to you from the beginning. Veil knew they'd pursue him and has been using you all as human shields. They don't want you; they want Veil. *Something* about him attracts them. Fox didn't say much because he couldn't but what he did tell me wasn't inspiring."

"So Fox is just their slave?"

"No doubt," Warden replies. "He's just an animal they befriended and allow to remain alive because he's intelligent enough to do their bidding, but not to challenge how humane it is."

"You don't think Veil's story about finding our stalker was his way to separate us from him; to save us from a fate he thinks he's heading for?" Amani asks, grasping at hope.

Warden stifles a laugh. "You're joking, right? He didn't run off to *save* you. He ran off to save himself. You got him so far. Now he can disappear and live in some underground ruins somewhere, off their radar."

"But who *are* they?" Chastity whispers.

Our group falls silent. Nobody knows and if they do, they dare not speak their name.

19

Elvandra Rae

There's an uncomfortable, sinister darkness in this part of the forest and it's creeping up on us the closer we get to the end of the trail.

Veil is continuously cursing to himself as he hacks at tangled weeds and overhanging branches, clearing an easier path for Donar and I. I'm beginning to tire and the grumbles of the forest's belly unnerve me.

I trudge too close to my Wardrobe companion and trip him but Donar only reaches out and squeezes my hand. The feeling– whatever it is- is mutual.

"Are we *any* closer?"

Veil hushes me. He hunkers low and edges a few steps ahead, then swings around and brings Donar and me to a sharp halt with an outstretched hand.

Stop, he's saying. There must be danger.

"I hear voices," Donar says. "Is that Eden?"

I open my mouth to shout for her; hearing her name is something I never thought I'd miss. Now I want to wrap my portrait-painting arms around the murderer's waist and squeeze.

Veil silences us and lowers his hood. Those piercing eyes are illuminated in the dim moonlight and they sparkle. How he blends so well into these surroundings strikes fear into my heart and suddenly I'm unsure hanging back with only Donar to protect me is wise.

Why would Veil not want us to rejoin our friends? Doesn't he trust them?

"I trust no one," he says, keeping his voice low and emotionless.

Donar startles and grabs me, forcing my body behind his so I almost can't see the teen.

"How did you know? What *are* you, a mutant?"

When Eden and the others are a safe distance away, Veil stands and removes his entire cloak, revealing his several layers of underclothing and patches of scar ridden skin. He begins a slow and steady pace toward us, his lids never blinking and his lips pursed, creating a light fog with every exhale. I feel as though we are being consumed by a shadow; something Hell spat out and sent to destroy the remnants of humanity.

"Veil, I don't care what you've done or what mutant gift you possess. Please let us take the food to our friends. Eden is sick. She needs it."

Veil laughs. "She is beyond help."

Donar tightens his grip. "Elvandra, you should run to them. They can't have gone far."

Veil takes a knife from one of his many layers and wipes it on his sleeve, clearing it of a dark-coloured substance. Donar gasps and drops his bag, then reaches for his own weapon, holding it at arm's length.

"Stay back. Veil, you saved our lives and brought us this far. I don't want to hurt you."

"Why betray us now?" I ask. "I thought we were friends."

Veil continues to creep, forcing us deeper into the forest and farther from the others. I wonder whose blood stains his sleeve and why he killed them. Did they provoke him or, as we have, try to help him? Until now Veil seemed such a gentle, if slightly damaged, adolescent. I was beginning to trust he'd take us all the way.

"You should not rely on your skull to contain such opinions, Elvandra." Veil grins. "As you know this is not my first time in the wild, nor will it be my last. I hear your curiosity and feel your fear and confusion. It buzzes like an unsatisfied itch or the beating of a passing insect's wings."

"If you don't like hearing the doubt why not face those questions with fact? Satisfy my curiosity. Convince me what you're doing is humane. Tell me, *what's going on?*"

"It is not humane," he admits, examining his knife and finally lowering those mesmerising eyes. "Still, I think before you die, I ought to explain what your sacrifice brings."

Donar loses his footing and together we clatter to the ground. Now we're completely helpless and the once small, harmless-looking teenager is a towering menace. We've lost the speck of control we relied upon so heavily. Panic sets in.

"When Czar released me, another less selfish community took me in. Sure I lost my friend and was devastated for a while, until I saw the truth of how weak the human race actually was in comparison to the grander, better evolved, more intelligent and technologically advanced species roaming our planet.

Their planet, now, but ownership of rock and weed is irrelevant.

"At first I feared them. They took samples of my saliva, my skin and my waste. Measuring every biological detail to figure out my strengths and weaknesses; what prompted tears, anger and fear. They fed me raw meat and fruit until my stomach could bear no more. When they were through studying me, speaking a language I could not understand and always in my presence, their leader tattooed me with these markings. I think it is their way to track me if within an ideal perimeter. They inserted a device here," he says, revealing a scar on his wrist. "We must be close. They sent a scout to find me."

"So you're not running from these people but toward them?" I ask, fumbling to hold my own weight in the melting snow.

"I am only running. This *is* what they wanted though; Czar especially, since making his deal. To release everyone; send them to collection zones for harvesting. Not I, though. I left their shelter to return to Titan. Their probes improved my communication skills. They *modified* me. I sense vibration and heat. I see the colours of your auras. Their tattoos guaranteed my safety. I realised my role was not to stay with them nor to die out here. My job was research. Through my eyes they studied our world."

"You're trading Titan's survivors? So it's not a race to live, it's a means to feed the enemy for your *own* freedom?"

"They are not our enemy but our superiors."

"Veil, all this time you've lived in Titan knowing

we'd never make it. How could you?"

"I am their eyes and ears into the human world, Rae. My brain is their encyclopedia. In return, I get to live."

Veil smiles; it's sinister and hideous but surprisingly comforting like although we are soon to die, it will be at the hands of a professional. Slick and painless.

"For so long humans believed we were the higher species. NORA, the meteor our government advised would wipe us from the face of this pathetic green planet, carried forth from another universe the Earth's saviours. Gods of the stars." Veil's arms raise as though he's praising the arrival of the apocalypse. "In exchange for my help, they will allow my survival if I return the data in good health. I plan to."

Veil lowers his skull so we can see the puncture marks, now healed but branded by circular star-shaped scars.

"Is that why you can read us?" Donar asks, scavenging discreetly for his dropped weapon. "They attached those probes to record your life and give you a means to record ours?"

I position my bag to give his wriggling fingers some shelter. Veil continues his dialogue, oblivious.

He nods. "The ability threw my concentration. My hood protected me from penetrating thoughts. I would integrate myself once more as a bug in Titan's shattering bottle and, at the ideal time when food and resources were at an all-time low and the Harmony Grid was close to activation, I would nudge it."

"So you can't be the only one then. Someone let those mutants in, didn't they?" I ask.

"Yes. Czar has been in on this for a while. His

Venturers discovered NORA long ago and have since tried to negotiate a peace treaty, which did not work. Why would it? Other than our slavery what did we have to offer them in exchange for such freedom?"

Veil grinds his teeth, then calms almost as quickly as the flame of his temper ignited.

"Still, it has been interesting observing you as they did me."

"Why NORA?" asks Donar, more in my direction than in Veil's.

Donar's palm meets his blade and I see the tension in his shoulders release. Now he can defend us should Veil decide we've heard too much.

"Not Of Rational Astronomy," Veil confirms, "is how the American government described the meteor before they realised its purpose. Their only rational astronomical explanation had been blown out of proportion by scientists who deemed a journey from across the universe impossible to survive and unrealistic. Aliens! For stories, said the critics, and then NASA became involved and attempted to build a 'meet and greet' ship to carry astronauts out to assess the danger. We had been hunting for life on other planets for so long, the idea of it occurring was beyond belief. Still, perhaps a friendship was possible; these beings intended us no harm. However, the Czars have been covering up this part of Earth's history for generations."

Veil pauses only to take a breath, then plunges right back into his story.

"All rational explanations became forgotten and instead, panic set deep into the heart of the political structure and cities began to fall. Nobody predicted such an apocalyptic scenario; all kinds of tsunamis and flooding and worldwide catastrophes. We gave up and agreed to die. Humans have never been very sustainable," he spits. "So now you know."

"About their arrival, sure, but not their *purpose*," I say, giving Donar time to form a plan. "I'd like to know what I'm about to die for. You owe me that much."

"I suppose. They plan to do this planet justice and re-build it," he says, brimming with pride and joy. "At least now I can say openly, without fear of being caught and crucified, that those banished inmates were in fact handed straight over to their soldiers. It is how I met them, too. My friend tried to save us at first but I was caught anyway.

"Czar let me back in because he too knew the truth and had been dealing in human trafficking for years already. It disgusted me until I settled into their frame of mind. Then it became an exciting challenge and something to live for when everyone else would die. A future I never expected to have in a world free from pollution and mutation as they promised."

"So *that's* their purpose here? To clean up? Seems like an awfully long, tiresome journey for the sake of fresh air." I say, but Veil doesn't react the way I'd hoped. "I can't understand why a kid as smart as you would believe this. They aren't even close to finishing the job. You'll die of old age first! You got us this far, Veil. Why save us only to kill us? Why act so human *all this time*?"

Veil, now bored of toying with our emotions, reaches down and grabs Donar by his throat.

"I promised I would take them some new study candidates, suitable to keep as pets for a little while, or as slaves. It is a shame you did not make the cut; Rachana might though with her natural mutations and Chastity, being so young, will make an interesting addition to their experimental inter-species breeding programme. With the proper training Eden can be broken to serve as I do."

"She'll resist you," Donar gasps. "They *all* will."

"I hope they do," he says. Veil throws Donar to the ground and raises his blade. "That is what makes my job so fun."

20

Ginny Bede

There's a piercing scream in the distance and Warden pauses only briefly to assess if it's worth returning to investigate. When he sets off running again I assume the answer is no.

Whomever the poor soul is, they're on their own. Death is a kinder fate on *Ad Infinitum* anyway.

We pelt through the snow at an incredible pace, especially with an injured inmate straggling along behind. I slow my sprint to help catch her up, then call forward to Warden to slow down. He forgets that although Eden holds a strong outer shell, inside she's human like the rest of us.

"Do you need a break?" I ask her.

"Is failure weakness?" she asks, and offers half a smile.

I fill her palm with Fox's pills and hope that although we can't be sure they're entirely good for her that they hold off the pain until we discover a new remedy. Warden promised he could find us a safe spot to spend the next twelve hours and that the grid is a pointless trip but after running for so long I'm beginning to doubt him.

"We'd be better making our own way now," he says. When we protest, he explains, "They have this entire area covered with scouts. I'd be surprised if they haven't already finished off our friends."

Before we pose further questions, Warden says he'll explain everything in detail as soon as we are off their radar. Fair enough, I reply, because unlike the others the adrenaline coursing through my veins is beginning to push me forward for a change. I even imagine replacing my usual alcoholic nightcap with it and surprise myself.

I smile at Eden and she smiles back, finally appreciating our help instead of blocking it. I'm still worried about her, though.

"Warden's eager to get us to shelter. Do you trust him?"

She shrugs. "More than Veil now. Warden has raised my suspicions and how could he leave you alone with the others hunting? Reckless behaviour is never respected, only feared. I should know. Most of the people I've encountered in my life have regretted meeting me. I'm dangerous and sadistic."

"I don't believe that," I reply, honestly, "nor do the others here. Do you think we'd have stuck with you for so long if we did?"

"Yes because you value your lives. I'm a recluse but of everyone here, Veil and I were your best bet, right?"

I nod but I'm not proud to admit she's right. I didn't choose Eden's company for her humour or anecdotes but rather her chances of survival. Perhaps it's not Eden at fault, but those surrounding her. Sometimes our behaviour not only defends our feelings but reflects them too, creating a way to spur their negativity.

I gesture at the others and advise we should probably catch up. Eden agrees and we stagger on together, keeping a steady pace for another hour. Warden calls us to a halt. There's a short drop down an overgrown hill to what appears to be an old subway entrance. There we can find shelter and warmth until Eden is at full strength again. Rachana is eager to examine the bite wound and Eden is eager to be given the all clear for mutation and infection, so we slide down the hill on our bottoms, leaving wavy trails in the snow.

When we finally get through the rusted barriers, down a couple sets of corroded stairs and into the tunnels, I'm relieved. I'd expected to see it thriving with mutated creatures like Titan's government had always explained and the Venturers had warned us of in training, but it's abandoned.

"Why hide in the darkness when this side of the Earth is dark for six months a year anyway?" Warden says. He gestures for us to get comfortable. "We're safe here for a while but there's no guarantee that predators won't follow our scent or tracks. If Veil's out there, he's going to find us eventually. If you see him *don't* try to reason. I promise you he'll arrive without company and give a sob story about how he tried to save Elvandra and Donar's lives, but it was too late."

We slump together using one another's body heat and drift to sleep. When we wake, the station is still as eerie and quiet as before but Eden isn't in her makeshift bed.

I sneak past the sleeping girls, pleased to see Rachana is snoozing peacefully and move carefully so I don't wake her. If I do she'll want in on my search for Eden. To risk her safety now we've found a safe place to hide would be ludicrous.

When I'm far enough down the tunnel, I whisper her name, allowing the echo of my voice to carry it further to the next station. There are shuffles and grunts. When she finally emerges, she's pale and her eyes are a piercing red. I rush to her side and catch her in time for the fall, grazing my knees on the old train lines.

"What happened?"

"I don't remember," she groans.

"Were you sleepwalking? Let's get you back to the others; give you more medication."

Eden takes my hand and squeezes. "I'm not going to make it, Ginny. They're making me worse."

"The painkillers Fox gave us? No, they're helping. Rachana said your wound isn't infected."

"What festers is deeper, Ginny. Leave me here; I'm a danger to you. Find Rae and Donar. Take Warden and figure out who these visitors are and destroy them. You're capable."

"Me? I'm just a trainer, Twelve. I'm no killer– not for a long time. My world revolves around my next drink and my brother. Both are gone. Now I'm a lost soul and you're our *only* guidance in a world where people like Veil rule all."

I pause and brush her hair back from her face, then plant a kiss on her cheek.

"You weren't sleepwalking, were you?" Eden shakes her head. Her eyes fill with tears. "Come on, don't give up on us now. We're not such poor company, are we?"

This raises a smile but it's cut short. "I'm frightened, Ginny. For the first time in my life, I'm terrified of my future. Being on death row was nothing in comparison to this inferno."

Eden coughs up blood and wipes her mouth on her sleeve, drawing away in fear.

"You're going to make it."

"I'm not well, Ginny. For as long as my behaviour is unpredictable you've got to restrain me. What if this bite changes me and I turn on you?"

"Well, I'll be sure to check for a foaming mouth. Now get up. I won't carry you. Stop this nonsense. I'll have Rachana treat the wound and wrap it in fresh bandages, then we'll find these people and reason with them. All right?"

"We should hear what Warden has to say about them first. Fox held him captive and those documents, although six hundred years old, so far support his accusations." Eden shudders. "Who *knows* what creeps and crawls down here."

"Warden's been right about the hideaway so far too. I suggest we trust him," I tell her. Eden smiles. "He's a good man and he loved you once. I think deep in that concrete heart of his is lingering magnetism."

"I sure hope so," she whispers. "I'm a free woman now and I'd like to stay that way, with or without him."

I aid Eden to her feet and mostly drag her back through the tunnel and on to the platform to meet Warden's criticising glare. He takes Eden's good arm and walks her back to bed, covering her in his stripped layers of clothing and then nudges Rachana. He doesn't have to explain why; she's on the case in seconds, cleaning and re-dressing the bite.

"I think it's starting to heal," she says, resting her hands on the arm gently and closing her eyes.

"It won't work," Eden says, hissing when Rachana's cool skin touches the wound. "You're special, kid, but your gifts are precious and limited behind that hardened shell of yours. Protect it. Don't share it, all right?"

Rachana frowns. "I was only trying-"

"You're not in trouble." She inhales deeply and shuffles beneath the blanket, struggling to find a comfy spot. "Does Veil know you can do that?"

"I think so."

Eden frowns. "Shame. He won't turn away easy. If you can, share it only with Ginny. He's your guardian and he loves you as his own daughter."

"We barely know one another," Rachana says.

Eden grins. "I see the way you look at him. Admittance isn't necessary. Thank you for dressing my wound, it feels much better now."

Rachana laughs. "Liar."

"Emotionally if not physically."

Then, she drifts off to sleep.

Warden calls a meeting. It's the perfect time to discuss Eden's health when she's asleep because she can't argue. Warden stomps on her suggestion to make these tunnels her permanent home. He's adamant that she needs constant care and this only reinforces my suspicion that he's still got feelings for her. Chastity, although young and beautiful, may have entertained him during their time apart but nothing breaks a strong bond like theirs. I see it in his eyes and the passionate way he speaks her name.

"Warden, what happened back at the sanctuary with Fox?" Amani asks him.

He wrings his hands together and grinds his teeth, infuriated by the mention of the ape's name.

"He's a pawn. Nothing more. Veil and Czar made a deal with the natives long before I became Warden. He's been feeding people to them for years. All this time I thought they'd get a shot at rebuilding a life or finding the Harmony Grid without our help but such a map has never really existed. Not how we thought."

"It's a trap then," Chastity says.

Warden doesn't have to answer because it's obvious by the clench in his jaw that our hope of finding a new home is gone.

"The Harmony Grid is a compound, built and heavily guarded by their soldiers. Those of us they capture and deem strong enough to serve them are imprisoned and, effectively replaced. From what I stole from the documentation, it's like they take refuge in your body, shoving you aside and borrowing the control of your limbs until they've completed their work, then they release you and place you into storage." He pauses. "In other words, you're a robot. That's where that weird glow comes from. It's them. You're their slave, literally controlled by their homicidal motives. NORA wasn't a meteor but a vessel, carrying them from afar to 'save' our planet from the species in control at the time.

"At first they tried to reason but our leaders weren't willing to share ownership and listen to their observations. They predicted that within another hundred years if they didn't take us down, we'd take ourselves down in a world-wide war ending in nuclear pollution and the release of biological warfare." Warden tries not to smile. "Look around you. It's clear we fought their influence for longer than the records show. So instead they decided we were more of a threat than a means to save Earth and our extinction could make way for life to begin again. These compounds were built all over the world, mostly at the equator. They figured that because of the planet's lack of rotation and the migration of the oceans to the poles, they'd be safest from flooding there. The structures of the grid are sanctuaries but for them, not us."

"With what purpose?" Amani asks.

"It protects them from the world as it currently stands until they can medicate it; nurse it to health and, presumably either live here themselves or move on."

"So they're just healers?" Rachana asks. "Like me?"

"That's an interesting comparison," Warden says, one eyebrow raised. "They held Veil for too long and experimented on him, probing his brain and enslaving him for some time. I once overheard a conversation between Veil and Czar but never registered the reference to this alien life force."

"Do you remember what they said?" I ask, "because it could help us figure out what Veil's plan is."

"Czar wanted to keep someone happy and away from Titan, so Veil agreed to identify people he felt might make good Venturers. He's recruiting, like a shepherd herds his sheep toward the safety of a pen. Only we're not sheep, we're human beings, and it's not a pen, it's-"

"I get it."

I cut Veil short because the image of hundreds of innocent Titan citizens being sifted and sorted to suit their needs or perhaps murdered if they're old or sick, disgusts me.

"We have to do something. How can we sit by and allow them to rule our planet?"

Amani says, "We can take it back."

"How?" asks Rachana. "We're kids, a middle-aged alcoholic and an inexperienced prison guard. No offence to anyone, of course."

"If you're going to insult me do it properly. Technically I'm a pensioner," I correct, and Rachana giggles. "So what's the next step, Warden? Do we know what's on each site?"

"Fox lives at their storage facility and it's marked with symbols so I'm presuming they speak little of our tongue."

"So how did they arrange to capture us with veil?"

"I don't know. Who knows what technology they have? Think how close humans were to breakthroughs in science before the apocalypse. Still, we use symbols like that too so it could be for camouflage," Warden says. "If any escapees stumble upon the buildings, it's to protect their identities. There are more, and I'm betting the location Zthora showed us on that map is their slaughterhouse."

"So the others are what?" Rachana asks. "Homes and offices?"

"Until we explore them we don't know. Personally," Warden says, "I think that the bigger the building, the more human-focused it will be. Prisons, living quarters, abattoirs."

"Which eliminates some, including Fox's building, so what about the others?" I ask.

"Labs and if they live here, underground hubs where they breed. To run such a huge operation requires manpower. I'm betting NORA couldn't accommodate all that at once. The Earth's been hit by meteors and comets before though, so how can we be sure they weren't walking and living among us for centuries?" Warden says. "Human clothing was thick enough back then to mask the glow."

His theory terrifies me. Our ancestors could have mated with, befriended and worked alongside these creatures. Our own genes may not be as pure as we believe. Perhaps that's why Rachana is gifted. Born from a long line of gradually enhanced humans with alien blood coursing through their veins rather than merely her father's. But if she can express empathy and sympathy, why can't they?

"Couldn't we try reasoning with them instead of attacking? Their weaponry is going to outrank our blunt blades and hand-made arrows. Like the prison batons," says Amani. "They were glowing electrical things. We can't fight without matching them."

"No," Warden says. "We survey the situation. If we can somehow get Veil to take us in as prisoners, we can infiltrate the compounds where Titan survivors are kept and bring them down. Veil has always wanted Czar dead ever since I've known him so whoever he works for must also want to eliminate Czar's influence. Why, I don't know, but perhaps if we get through to Czar we can use him to our advantage."

"As a hostage?" asks Chastity.

"If they don't care about his death they won't value a hostage but he knows an awful lot about them. Veil dislikes him for a reason. I'll bet he's in on security too, and their plans and history. If anything, they'll want to be rid of him to remove evidence. They've made use of him; his people are scattered and Titan is dead. If I didn't know better, I'd say there are lots of Titan-like structures all over the Earth that they've infiltrated and sabotaged. Yet another pawn in a complex game of chess."

"So what do you suggest our next step is?" Amani says.

Warden stands, stretches and then scratches his chin. He glances over at Eden and sighs.

"I don't know. I'm out of ideas."

Rachana clears her throat. "I have a suggestion. Send Chastity and I in with Eden; let Veil witness us hand ourselves openly to what we assume is Czar's new sanctuary. She's injured and we need help, so they'd have to keep face and let us in. Right?"

"Kid's got a point," Warden says.

"Once we're inside we can begin gathering basic intel. Who they are, what they're doing here. When we're done and they trust us we'll release the prisoners and cause chaos. If he does see us, with Veil distracted he's not interfering. I'm your best bet because if I get injured, I'll heal."

"If you're not killed," I reply. "I'm not so sure."

"Ginny, you know I'm capable."

"Look, no offence to Chastity, but we can't rely on her to fight off a threat. You're better used for your innocent face and your youth, right?" Warden tells her. She smiles and nods. It's probably the nicest thing he's ever said to her. "Rachana can hold her own."

"Sure I can. For Eden."

"What about the others? Elvandra and Donar?" Chastity asks. "I liked them, they were nice."

"They were good, honest people, but there's no time to go back for them. If they're alive they're on their own for now. If this whole thing is a success we can search for them later." I tell her.

She nods but I can tell she isn't completely satisfied we'll make it out alive. If not, we're all dead anyway, including our friends from Wardrobe.

Warden sets off toward Eden and pops open her pills.

"I think we have a plan now," I tell him. "And it just might work!"

Warden smiles. "That's about the best thing I've heard you say to date, Ginny ol' pal."

21

Elvandra Rae

Red ink splatters across my face, burns a line in the snow and then dissipates as it hits the leaves of a nearby tree. I'm up and running, leaving behind my gear and provisions before Donar takes his last breath. With his throat slit and Veil's wrath still upon him, I already know there's no chance he'll survive. Donar wouldn't want me to hang around and give Veil the chance to take a second victim.

My job now is to warn the others.

When Donar collapsed upon me, my ankle twisted beneath me and now causes an uncomfortable limp. Although I'm in little pain, it's distracting, like a stone in my shoe or an itchy collar. The longer I put weight on the strain, the slower I'll run and with a natural born killer on my heels, it's a wound I can't afford.

I lunge through the trees, caring not about mutants, ice, predators or becoming lost, only about the crazed, blood-thirsty teenager I hear rustling behind me. My lungs begin to burn, my legs throb and the weight of each layer of clothing, even without the supplies strapped to my back or my drawings to carry, are a burden.

Veil doesn't say anything; he doesn't need to shout abuse and threats to scare me. I'm already as terrified as I deem possible and eager to find somebody– *anybody*– who is willing to help me fight off this monster. I'm doing well. In fact, I've almost outrun him enough to find a place to hide until he passes, unbeknownst to my temporary sanctuary until I trip and fall on my face. The snow soaks my hair, seeps down the back of my neck and wets my clothes. I'm instantly freezing and less inclined to fumble to my feet.

Veil emerges behind me. His blade is still blood stained and now as he aims it at my chest, I take what I believe will be my final breath.

"Hey!"

Veil spins at the sound of an unfamiliar voice and is knocked unconscious by a thick fallen tree branch, wielded by Mika and her married mentors. Pregnant and clumsy though she may be, I thank whatever god may be watching over us for her perfect timing.

"Elvandra, is that you? Where's Donar?"

I can't help myself. I sob until my body is unable to produce tears and each inhale becomes a dry, squawking heave. Mika kneels beside me, hands me her canteen and insists I use the remainders to wash my face of Donar's blood and swill out my mouth.

"*How* are you still alive?" I ask her.

Mika glances at her mentors who are securing Veil's wrists with rope and smiles.

"Terrain experts, remember? You look awful, Elvandra. Weren't you with others?"

"How do you know that?" I ask, my eyes wide, although puffy and red. "Have you seen my friends?"

"Not since we noticed you hiding in the tower. Corrina's death spurred us on. Until then we'd planned to climb and meet you. We had no choice but to escape before the beast turned on *us*." She pats her belly and hums. "I think they are beyond mercy and compassion even for an expectant mother."

"Are there more of you?" I ask.

Mika aids me to a more dignified stance. She offers me a tissue to blow my nose and pulls me into an embrace. She doesn't reply, but part of me is pleased with the silence. I can't take any more death. Not today.

"Donar was a good man," she says after a while. "Withdrawn and sad, but kind-hearted."

"He always protected me," I reply, gathering my dropped things and pausing to give Veil a good kick in the ribs. He's still unconscious and so doesn't notice but it makes me feel better. "This psychopath murdered my only real friend."

Mika pauses until I've composed myself. "We saw Czar leave Titan, you know."

"When?"

She shrugs. "Without a sunrise I can't predict an exact time. I'd say about six or seven hours ago. We stayed close to the complex for a while in hope of returning to find shelter and security in the infirmary, to prepare for the baby. My husband was crushed by a collapsed roof on our way out; I could barely see through my tears but Czar's a distinctive fellow. I couldn't miss him. The guards didn't pause to help us, nor did the governor. They continued along their own selfish path toward the closest exit, right where you guys left. That's why we followed."

"But we never saw Czar leave," I reply. "The watchtower gave us a grand view of Titan's compound and if they escaped around the same time Corrina was murdered, then-"

Suddenly it hits me like a brick to the skull. Perhaps that's why we were set upon by that mutant humanoid; a distraction to free the one person Titan's citizens really cared about.

Daemon Czar.

"Is Czar in on this? Did he let in the banished?"

Mika shrugs. "Don't know much anymore, not for sure anyway. I won't trust powerful people, especially since witnessing Veil's insanity. What drove him to such *madness*?"

"Veil's one of them," I tell her.

"Who, Czar's guards? Veil *hated* Czar. I've heard him curse the name before."

I take the opportunity to tell Mika and her mentors everything whilst Veil sleeps, remembering to mention the meat hidden in our packs and Eden's wound. Mika cringes when I describe the attack but can't understand why Veil saved Eden's life when all along he'd planned to hand her over to murderous aliens anyway.

"Aliens; it's such science fiction," Mika says. "I can't believe NORA wasn't just a ball of rock like the reports and history books documented. Did the government really cover up such a strange disaster?"

I nod. "And more. The Harmony Grid isn't a sanctuary but their compound. Veil worked for them all along, developing our skills and using those weaker to maintain Titan until they were ready to receive us. The whole point of Titan's destruction was to round up those strong enough to survive in the wilderness and use us to their advantage."

Mika swallows hard and begins to sweat, even in the falling snow.

"As food?"

"As slaves, for food, for reproduction, experimentation. You name it, they've considered it. Veil told us the whole story before he attacked Donar. He never predicted I'd run. Now he's tied up and no longer a threat, my priority is to retrieve my abandoned belongings and find my friends. Chastity, Warden, Eden, Ginny and the kids are all out there somewhere."

Mika takes my hand. "We'll help you, right guys?"

Her mentors smile and nod but are still pondering what to do with our prisoner. Veil could make good leverage if my friends are captured. He's on the enemy's side now, after all, and if they learn he's alive and captured, they might send scouts to search for him. Either to rescue him and eliminate us or to end his life to be sure he can't talk.

It's a little late for that, though. Villains always spill the gossip before they attempt to murder you.

"You're very kind but this isn't your fight and it's too dangerous. I'm so sorry about your husband."

"What else is there to do now?" Mika asks. "If we go back, we'll be killed. If we go with you, we may be captured and enslaved or worse! If we head on alone we may never see another human being again."

"At least you'll be alive," I tell her. "To raise your child."

"In this world I'm not sure it's worth the try."

Mika is saddened knowing her child will grow up

without a father or a stable home. How can she care for a crying baby in a world where the slightest noise can attract claws, teeth and aliens?

"Head back to the watchtower, it's safest there," I tell them. "Don't follow the map Czar gave us. When I find my friends we'll check it out and hopefully cause some trouble to slow down their hunt of our community. Then we can all move on together."

"I hear the oceanic ruins are worth seeing," Mika says, smiling. "The receded waters revealed all kinds of wreckages and treasures the ocean once swallowed. Ships, submarines and the bones of animals which have been extinct for hundreds of years. There must be places we can hide there."

"So it's a deal then," I tell her. "When it's safe and our work is done, we'll come back for you. I promise. Then we can all travel together to the oceanic ruins and wait for the sun."

I shake Mika's hand and thank her once again for saving my life and putting her own in danger, then walk back a short while to find my pack. I hand it over and explain that inside she'll find deer, clothing, water and weapons and that when Veil wakes they should tie him somewhere he can't be of any danger to himself or others. If he dies there, so be it. I'll require revenge one day but unlike Veil, I have a conscience.

When they're gone I crouch in the snow for a few moments and gather the courage to continue on this journey alone. I have no tracking skills, no hunting skills, no companion to comfort me or keep me from going crazy. It's freezing out here and dangerous; the blood on my clothing will attract all kinds of predators by scent. But there isn't enough time to worry. Whatever happens is now unavoidable and deemed my fate. If there's a creator or higher being, I pray they will care for me and my friends until we're reunited.

With my drawings rescued and the memory of Donar embroidered beautifully at the back of my mind, I stand and take my first independent step into the unknown.

22

Eden Maas

I'm the first to emerge from the abandoned subway station.

We are each greeted with a beautiful sight or sensation we hadn't noticed before. The sleep, food and security, however brief, has rested us plenty and our eyes are open to the tasks at hand.

Above us are stars splattered on a cloudless navy canvas. The leaves of the forest rustle gently in the cool breeze, pointing the way to Czar's false sanctuary with their tips. It's like they're speaking to me. Some in warning when the wind picks up and they panic, but others with grace and best wishes as they sway, calm and relaxed, waving us by.

Our footsteps thud against the earth, waking smaller animals and scattering them as we pass. In a world unfamiliar with a human presence, they appear more afraid of us then we are of them and I can't blame their precautions. History has proven we're not as good-natured as we believe. We waged wars and broke laws instead of respecting one another and living in harmony. Perhaps the apocalypse would never have happened; these aliens may never have identified Earth to be in need of an intervention.

"Are we on course?" I ask Warden.

"Let me worry about the map. How are you feeling after last night's outburst?"

"You overheard my conversation with Ginny?"

Warden shrugs. "Some of it. Can't say I blame you and my better half owes you both a thanks and an apology." He pauses to take a sip from his canteen, then continues. "A thanks for your concern; you were willing to split from the group to avoid harming us. Proves there are good people left on *Ad Infinitum* after all."

"And the apology?" I prompt.

"Oh, about your book." Warden cringes. "I lost it when Fox knocked me out. It's our only copy so I feel guilty."

I reach into my bag and retrieve the dirt and blood-stained copy of Dante, then tap him on the shoulder. Warden's eyes light with joy and his hands caress it, then meet mine in thanks. We stand in silence, staring at one another, until Ginny clears his throat and points between the trees ahead.

On the horizon is a prison-like structure with barbed wire and a watchtower, guarded by a silhouette.

"Is that one of them?"

"Most likely in human form given they're expecting guests, but yes. See the glow?" Warden sighs. "Are you sure about this, Eden? We can go back or continue on."

"I'm no saint," I tell him, "but I can't ignore this."

When we're a little closer, the snow begins to fall again, heavier this time, and it makes walking difficult. Our feet disappear, using our energy to trudge a path to their gate. The guards point weapons at us, but they're unlike any I've seen on this planet before, from experience and research. Appearing as long, silver rods, these weapons glow orange as though they've been toasting over a campfire. I fear their touch like I feared my guard's baton.

I wrap my arms around Warden's neck and linger there, inhaling the scent I once took comfort in and then release to take the hands of two children. Ginny hangs back, holding Warden's things as he says goodbye, then calls to him. If they don't leave us now, they'll be spotted and most likely captured with us.

I close my eyes as they disappear, wanting to hold onto their memory, then rap on the gate with my good arm. It slides open seconds later, revealing a snow-covered compound with several human guards milling in and out of smaller blocks.

They look like the barracks of an army base and as I look a little closer, I see it probably once was exactly that. There are bullet holes in the walls and collapsed enclosures that are guarded in certain places to be sure their security is not breached. As the gates slide closed behind us, I shudder at the possibility that I may never see the other side of them again.

"Hello," says a bland male voice. The owner outstretches a gloved hand and shakes Rachana's firmly. "Congratulations, you made it across the Harmony Grid in time. Did you explore any of the other venues before arriving here?"

Chastity shakes her head. If we disclose our visit to Fox's facility, they'll presume we've also seen and released Warden. Word will surely have spread that he's missing by now and if Fox isn't within these walls somewhere, he'll be out looking.

"I'm sorry to hear it, there were extra provisions there. Czar's venturers ensured they were well stocked and secure, although we weren't quite prepared for the sudden evacuation of Titan. Our plans were implemented a little early this time around."

The man pauses, realising he may have revealed information we weren't supposed to know, but then continues hoping our minds are too exhausted to notice. But *I* noticed. They've done this all before, meaning Warden's predictions that Titan wasn't the only underground ark remaining is correct.

If they haven't emptied them yet, we must make it our priority to seek their location and pre-warn them all.

"We're pleased you made it. Not long until the gates are locked for good. In fact, in approximately five hours we'll do just that. This way please."

We follow the man across the yard to the first building, which is so small I figure it must lead to an underground corridor. When he opens the door, I'm right. There is a tiny office where a man is asleep with his feet on the desk, and some stairs leading down to a dank cellar.

Once we're through the door there will be no turning back no matter my excuse. I can't tell them I'm claustrophobic. I've lived in Titan all my life.

"Where are you taking us?" Chastity asks.

The man turns and points at my wound when we reach the final step. "The infirmary. We'll take care of your friend's bite."

"How did you know-"

"I assumed. Many of the others arrived with flesh

missing. *Ad Infinitum* is a vile place to live; we're not sure many more will arrive in time."

The man walks us down a narrow corridor lit by candles and then through some double doors. There are twelve metal slabs lined in the centre. Some are occupied with corpses and others with survivors. He's right, they are all either wounded or dead, and I'm about to join them.

"I will leave you in the capable hands of Shone. She's a medic and can patch up your bite."

I swallow hard. "Before you go, can you tell me if my friends are here? The Warden, a kid called Amani and a man named Ginny Bede?"

The man frowns and shakes his head. "I'm sorry. I haven't greeted anybody by those names."

"How about Donar and Elvandra? They worked in Wardrobe." Rachana takes my hand and squeezes it gently in anticipation, but the answer is the same. "Thank you anyway," she says and then the man leaves. "Worth a shot. At least now they can't tie us to Warden and Ginny."

I wink but am forced to lay on the end slab before we can discuss our tiny victory further. Shone takes off my top layers and unravels the bandage, then grunts and groans as she examines the wound. Rachana and Chastity are permitted to stay by my side so long as they don't try to interfere, and they're watching her every breath to be sure she doesn't try anything.

Shone seems reasonably normal. I'm not convinced she knows much about the true rulers of this establishment.

"You were bitten by what?" she asks, reaching for a

bowl of water and some fresh bandages.

"Not sure. A humanoid, I think. It walked like a human but had the muzzle of a wolf and the paws of a lion. It moved like an ape. Is there a scientific name for such a creature?"

Shone shakes her head. "We just refer to them as class B mutants."

"As opposed to?" Rachana prompts.

Shone raises a brow and shoos the kids back a few steps.

"To class A and C."

"I'm unfamiliar with the references," I tell her.

It's the truth, too. In Titan, you were either human, banished or mutant. There were no in-betweens.

"Class A mutants are those born without human emotion or rationality. Completely lost to all chances of communication and are focused only on food. I'd say the majority of Titan's population were killed by a class A. Class B," she continues, "are like the beast you fought. They are half-human and half-animal. They look like us sometimes but no longer act like us. Radiation and pollution likely prompted their evolution," she explains. "Then there's class C, which is what you are."

"I'm sorry?"

Shone straps my relaxed arms down to the slab and warns the girls to stay back. I writhe for a short while, arguing that I feel fine and am by no means mutant as I've lived inside all my life. I'm no more a mutant than she is, I reason.

"Not yet, but you will be. When bitten by a class B, you are likely to inherit the temperament of a class B. You may not change physically but you *are* infected."

Aeon Infinitum: Run For Your Life

Shone lowers her head and uses a magnifying glass to examine my wound before she wraps it tight in a fresh bandage.

"These green lines mark the beast's DNA in your blood. So far it has only reached your shoulder, so if we amputate the arm now we may be able to save the rest of you."

Chastity begins to cry. "Please don't hurt her."

"Oh it won't hurt one bit," she promises the girl. "I'll remove the arm, and when she wakes it will all be over. Titan only permits healthy, capable humans so you'll be asked to leave upon recovery. We have another compound three miles North of here. I'll warn you in advance, it's an unpleasant structure. I believe it is the remainders of an old insane asylum." She pauses, "So, shall we get this over with?"

23

Eden Maas

They're going to amputate my arm. They're going to amputate my arm. They're going to amputate my arm.

My eyes widen at Rachana and Chastity. My body is stiff and far from accepting; how can I survive out there with one arm? It leaves me no option but to go to their sanctuary and be forever in their debt for saving my mutant life.

Rachana shakes her head. "I don't think it's a good idea, Shone. Our survival relies on *all* our limbs."

Shone ignores her protest and tightens the straps around my arm. She picks up a syringe, taps the end, and promises this will be over before I know it.

"Didn't you hear me?"

"I heard you," Shone says, "but I must do what is in the best interests of my patient, even if she refuses to cooperate."

"There's got to be another way," I ask, struggling to pull free before she can stick me with the needle. "Please, I beg you."

I have never begged for anything before; not in Titan and not since being released. No matter how hungry, thirsty, cold, sick or emotionally unstable I was,

I have *never* pleaded for my life before. Now it seems even though the words have finally passed my lips, it will be like I hadn't bothered.

Shone jabs my arm with the needle and plunges a light blue fluid into my vein, then feeds me two pills. For a while I feel fine, but then my vision becomes blurred and the room begins to spin. I hear Rachana arguing and a clatter of Shone's metal instruments and although I'm conscious enough to realise she's trying to free me and being restrained, I can't balance well enough to help her.

"Eden, you have to run!"

Rachana's voice echoes. I'm seeing three of her. She's shaking me violently by the shoulders and Chastity is fumbling with my restraints.

"Go, now!"

The girls haul me off the slab and march me down the corridor and into another room.

"Where's the doctor?" I ask, stammering every word.

"Got a taste of her own medicine," Rachana says.

She throws me through a wooden door and into a dimly lit room. I'm so light-headed I can't make out much, except for small square screens on the far wall which appear to be computers or televisions. Other than in history books, Titan inhabitants haven't seen technology like this in a long time. If I try to reach out I find my arm is limp and pain-free.

"She drugged me," I whisper, except I've probably announced it louder than expected. "What did she give me?"

"I don't know."

Aeon Infinitum: Run For Your Life

Chastity slams a tin cup of water on the table and tips white grains into it. She swills it around and tips my head back, then pours it down my throat.

"Is this going to work? It's only salt," Chastity says.

Rachana nods. Immediately I feel sick and empty the contents of my stomach at the base. Rachana slaps my cheek and orders I do it again.

"Whatever those pills were, we'll flush them out," she says. "Stay here."

Rachana leaves, prompting chaos to erupt in the corridor. There are heavy footsteps and gunshots, then the sound of lightning cracking and a scream. Chastity's eyes widen. I'm coming around enough to get my bearings back and the feeling in my arm. I steal a glance at the discoloured strings in my blood and can see, exactly as Shone said, the infection is spreading. The fluid she injected seems to be attacking it and I feel wriggles of action beneath my skin.

"Is she *insane*?" Chastity mutters.

"Where's she gone?"

"I think she's distracting them so we can escape."

"That's not the plan," I say, rubbing my head and releasing my hold on the table for the first time, hoping I can stand upright.

The lights were indeed computer screens marked with strange symbols in a language I can't understand. I reach out and push a few buttons but there's no sound and nothing happens. I must need a password. I point to a cabinet in the corner and tell Chastity to rummage for anything we can use to get Rachana back; something that looks important or valuable. Maybe they'd be willing to trade for her life.

Chastity begins pulling files from the cabinet, flicks through and then discards them on the floor. Within minutes it is covered in white paper but she returns empty-handed.

"Nothing I can understand, Eden. We need to go, now. Whilst they're chasing her we can find the prisoners and free them."

"We don't even know they're here," I reply. "We're completely reliant on luck. Not to mention Veil. We have no idea where he is or if he's alive. We should never have split up."

This was a terrible idea. Sure Rachana can heal quickly but she's never tested if her mutant blood will resurrect her from death. How did I let myself get into this situation? Being bitten, dragged into a compound, drugged and then left to be the irresponsible one? Why did a teenage girl have to take matters into her own hands to save my life? And that awful crack of lightning! Are those rods a form of taser? For all we know she's been electrocuted and thrown in a cell.

I creep to the door with Chastity, still feeling dizzy and queasy, but I have to plough on. Chastity is right behind me, holding me steady and carrying our things because the extra weight throws my balance. We peep through the door; the corridor is empty and the door to the stairwell is open. There are echoes of voices and a trail of blood disappearing around the corner. I sincerely hope it's not Rachana's and if it is, that she's already healing and found her way out of this tomb.

"Come on, it's clear."

We run back to the exit and out into the compound. There are human guards in the distance and at once, as though controlled, they turn and march in a line toward us. It's obvious we're escapees because we're red in the face, sweaty and injured. Everyone else at the sanctuary appears healthy and clean. But before the line reaches us, with only a hundred yards to spare, there are shouts from the nearest collapsed wall and Warden, led by Ginny and the pregnant Wardrobe worker Mika, pile through.

They take out the first guard and stampede over the second before their illuminated rods are raised. Warden retrieves one on his way in and they wave at us to join them.

"Quick!" Mika yells, "we're out of time."

"Where's Rachana?" Ginny asks.

We're too busy running from the ever closer line of aliens to answer. All I can do is shake my head and hope he doesn't think she's dead. As we speed up, so do the guards and they raise their rods, preparing to strike.

"Well that didn't work now, did it?" Warden says. I can only frown at him and concentrate on not falling over. "I cannot *believe* I let you lead them inside."

"This was *Rachana's* idea," Ginny reminds him. "Not Eden's, and they've clearly done something to her. She can barely stand."

Ginny takes my arm and leads me behind one of the outbuildings.

"Do you have any idea where they took her?"

I shrug and gesture at Chastity who tells them the story. Rachana left of her own accord so we could get out of that place before they chopped off my limb, most likely to feed it to their alien friends. I'm grateful to her, alive or dead.

"Where did *you* come from?" she asks Mika.

She's accompanied by her two mentors from Wardrobe who are firing at the line of guards and only occasionally striking one of them. I'm concerned we're firing at human beings; they're not capable of kicking out the aliens occupying their minds.

Instead of shooting them we ought to be freeing them if we can figure out how.

"We found Elvandra," Mika replies. "Veil murdered Donar but Elvandra managed to run away. We got there just in time to knock him out. He's tied up in the watchtower back at Titan. Elvandra said we should go and wait for her there and we did for a while, but when she never came back we thought it better that we help."

"Those weapons though," I manage. "They're *ancient*."

"Well, humans haven't made weapons like this since the apocalypse. They're museum pieces we retrieved."

"Titan's not completely dead, then?" Chastity asks, mopping my brow and handing me Fox's pills. "You got in and out without issue?"

"Not exactly," she says. "We came down from the tower and were chased back to the silo. Veil's tool was still lodged in the door so we slid under and released it. Some of the corridors were collapsed but there's a clear path from there to the weapons room in Wardrobe. These were all that remained. The rest were looted."

"They're getting closer," Ginny says. "We need to move. We should forget about the others, there's no time."

"We can't leave Rachana behind," I tell him. "She saved my life. You guys should find where they're holding our people. I'll distract them."

Warden peers at our attackers and shakes his head. Sweat drips from his forehead. All this running through the snow, shooting at our enemies, has increased our body heat in an ice-covered world. The thought almost makes me laugh.

"This bite will only get worse, Warden," I tell him. "I'll become aggressive and I don't want to hurt those I love. Despite everything I've grown to kind of like you guys."

I place my palm against his face and direct him to Chastity and Mika.

"They need a leader. If I'm to die at least let me go out a hero."

"It's not going to be smooth and pain-free," Ginny says. "Surely if you come with us we'll find a way to prevent the bite festering?"

"Other than amputation there's no other way, and I'm useless to everyone then. This world doesn't welcome the sick, Ginny, it destroys them. At least here I'm in control of how I die. Out there, I'm a meal." The line is almost upon us. "Now go, it's alright. Find our friends and get them out. I'll hold them off for as long as I can."

The others each say goodbye in their own way. Mika squeezes my hand, Chastity hugs me and Ginny pats me firmly on the back, careful to avoid sending vibrations to my bad arm. Warden approaches and at first, I think he's about to try to talk me out of it, but then his lips are on me and our noses bump. It's the most intimate moment I've had since before Czar's attempted assassination, and as a final memory, it's kind and exciting.

"I'm sorry," he whispers, hands me my bow, and then they're gone.

I step out, armed with arrows and bite my lip as the pain in my arm becomes so excruciating I'm not sure I'll hit my target. I take a shot and hit the end guard's leg, knocking him to his knees. He stares blankly at it, angered by the inconvenience of being unable to walk but barely registering the pain or the blood. I wonder if the human he's stifling inside is screaming in agony and if so, I reason it's kinder than aiming for the head.

I'm thankful for my training days, preparing me for this moment. At the time I never imagined I'd be buying my friends time to escape an alien threat. I only hope they free as many captured Titan citizens as possible and get the hell out of here before the complex comes down.

It's up to me to do that, but not yet. If I can give them thirty minutes to fight, I can die satisfied.

I hunker low and slide out again, hitting the second guard in the shoulder and knocking him back. He staggers and drops his weapon. It's not much of a success but one less threat for now. In the corner of my eye, I spot Chastity's blonde hair disappear into a large building which appears to be a cell block. At least they made it out of the open.

I've killed two and injured another six, leaving three guards still armed and two in the watchtower overlooking the exit. I'm breathless and my arm is sore, but I have one bent arrow left to fire and I need to make it count.

The next step will be a cross between bravery, stupidity and suicide when I charge at them with my

Aeon Infinitum: Run For Your Life

knife.

Before I retrieve my arrow and take aim, there's a huge explosion in the compound which takes out two of the armed guards and snaps the wood at the base of the watchtower. I can't believe how slow it topples, but when it does there's no way the watchmen have survived the fall.

Rachana charges from the smoke and fire, armed with nothing more than her bare hands and throws her body at the final guard, wringing his neck from behind. Although she's helped me, I take aim and step out from behind the wall.

"Get up."

Rachana does as I ask and holds up her hands. Her face is badly burned and her clothing is charred down one side, but other than evidence from the explosion she appears unharmed.

"It's me," she says.

"How do I know? Prove it!"

Rachana drops her gear, inches toward me and says, *"Do not be afraid; our fate cannot be taken from us; it is a gift."*

She throws her pack at me and gestures at the contents. When I look down I find it is filled with documents and files marked SECRET.

Rachana smiles. "Eden, it's me. Lower your bow."

24

Warden

The cell block is in worse condition than Titan's.

It is strewn with human excrement, plagued by rats and is dank and mould-infested. By stepping foot inside it I feel instantly filthy and cannot imagine how Titan's survivors have lasted so long here.

They crouch in their cells which are so small they may as well be kennels or cages; the women are in tears and the men are so busy trying to claw their way free they barely notice our presence.

At the end of the corridor, I see a large lever which I recognise from Titan to be the means to open every cell at once. We only use it for lunch, work and exercise times or if we're banishing an entire block under Czar's orders.

"Warden, how fitting you should be drawn to the cell block."

I startle and spin on my heel to find Czar on the platform overhead with his hands around the throat of Elvandra Rae. I shove my friends aside and step closer.

"Let her go, Daemon."

Czar bellows and grabs Rae by her hair, then shoves her to the top of the metal stairs he stands beside. He kicks the backs of her knees until she crumples, then dangles her forward.

"Kill him!" she screams.

"Shut up!" Czar growls. "Can't you see how pathetic humans are, Warden? I thought if I groomed you well enough you'd be suited to stand beside us when we ruled *Ad Infinitum* together."

"*Us?*" I ask. "You and what army, Czar?"

"Veil, of course. You *must* have figured out his involvement by now?"

Mika drops her gear and steps forward. "Veil's dead, Daemon. We tied him to the watchtower and left him. He murdered Donar in cold blood. Let Elvandra go. She's of no use to you now."

Czar grins and kicks Elvandra's back, launching her forward. She is knocked unconscious on the metal railing. Her body tumbles to the bottom where she lands in a heap.

Mika kneels by her side and takes her pulse. The colour drains from her face.

"She's gone, Warden."

Ginny ushers Mika and Chastity away from the body, then drags her aside. He pauses to mourn her. Here, in the centre of the first floor, she's displayed for all to witness Czar's power. Elvandra deserves more than that.

Ginny sits her against an empty cell and brushes her hair back, then drapes his jumper over her face. Moments later he's by my side with clenched fists and narrow eyes.

"She never harmed anyone!" he yells.

"So with that playful inmate of yours, your friends

from Wardrobe and the little mutant girl you've been so accepting of wiped from the face of this planet, it leaves a rather pathetic, powerless group of misfits left to conquer me." Czar laughs and begins to descend the stairs toward Ginny and I. "Tell me, how do you plan to defeat the new rulers of Earth? Can't you see how beneficial my plan is to the re-population of our little blue planet?"

"It's not blue anymore, not since *they* crashed into it with NORA," I reply. "It's sick, believing you can decide who lives and dies to create the perfect community and begin again. We're a dying species and you're willing to wipe half of us out because we're not strong enough or fast enough to play your games. The Harmony Grid brought hope to so many and it was all a lie."

"It was a means to please a higher being."

"What, these *aliens*?" Ginny's voice increases in volume and as Czar nears us, he begins to close the gap too. I reach out to stop him. "Warden, let me go. This man murdered hundreds of innocent men, women and children to satisfy the needs of a species that stole our planet. Time can heal the Earth and until then we need to be patient, not allow nosey neighbouring spacemen to interfere. We made our bed," he tells Czar, "so we'll lie in it until the Earth heals naturally."

"And if it doesn't?" Czar asks. "What are your plans, Ginny? Are you going to banish my friends and send away the only hope of this planet's survival?"

"Why not?" I reply. "That's what you did to Titan. Sacrificed Titan's only hope of survival: its people. Those who have grown your food, made your clothes, explored your planet and shared your bed. Your ancestors had plans for Titan, Daemon, and I cannot imagine they wanted you to share an alliance with those responsible for the apocalypse."

"We've known for hundreds of years about our *friends*," Czar explains. "The evidence is clear and in safe storage, and they are not aliens. They are as human as we are. Your girl, for example, Ginny. Her parents were killed defending her gift. It skipped generations I'm afraid, but her grandmother carried the blood of our visiting species. They have monitored the Earth for thousands of years, watching the human race destroy all that is pure and now they plan to nurture it back to life, minus its current population."

My eyes catch a glimpse of two silhouettes entering the block behind Czar's platform. As they creep nearer and Czar continues his inspirational speech about how wonderful his new friends are and what they can offer, I begin to make out the fiery red hair of young Rachana and the laboured steps of Eden.

"Enough of this."

Ginny shakes his head and jogs to the lever, pulling it down with all his might and opening up the cell doors to release our people.

"It's time for the true lovers of this planet to take back their home. You can't enslave us or use us for vessels any longer, and something tells me that the Daemon Czar your father raised, to be honest, is stifled somewhere in the brain you've stolen."

Czar's eyes light beautifully, like two stars in the darkness and as he opens his mouth, from it escapes a beam so bright I am forced to shield my eyes.

Eden and Rachana make their move, lunging to

disarm him and knock him to the ground, pinning his body to the dirty floor. Czar fumbles and kicks the girls off, muttering about how stupid they were for believing it was really him all this time and Veil, he insists, is innocent too. It takes all my self-containment not to kick him in the ribs and crush his fingers beneath my boot as punishment for murdering Elvandra, but if he's telling the truth he may not have had control of his body.

"Where did he go?" Rachana asks, helping Titan's citizens out of their cells and directing them to the nearest exit. "Did he leave?"

Ginny shakes his head and helps Eden and Czar to their feet. "I doubt it. They have as much claim to this planet as us now. They've lived here almost as long, although their proof is thin. This isn't the end."

Czar coughs and straightens his clothing, infuriated. "He's moved on to another body. You'll never catch him now. A few miles from here there's a storage facility guarded by a mutant their leader enslaved. They call him-"

"Fox," I say. "Yes, we've met. *Lovely* guy."

"I'm sorry," Czar said. "He's under orders from their leader- from me- I mean from the alien who took refuge within me that is, to guard those documents and kill anyone who stands in his way. He was to bring any humans who strayed too close to this facility for branding and slavery." Czar blinks and shakes his head. "It feels so spacious and free in here now, I can think for myself again."

"I'm pleased for you," I tell him with less excitement than it probably deserves. "Can you help Eden? She was bitten by a mutant and told the only way to save her would be amputation."

"I'm afraid that's correct. There's nothing I can do," Czar says.

Eden pinches the bridge of her nose and shakes her head, then decides his presence is too infuriating and leaves the cell block, taking Rachana and Chastity with her.

"I'm sorry for your friend," Czar says.

"She's strong, she'll pull through," I tell him. "Can you at least offer us a burial for Elvandra's body?"

"That I think I can manage," he says, "and considering she died by my hands, it's the least I can do."

25

Eden Maas

The fresh air clears my head.
I know what I have to do.
So many have died because of the will of others that it would be unfair of me to expect my friends to live with the monster I'll become. If I can guard and watch over them from afar, in whatever form this infection will produce, then I'll settle for simply knowing they can live in peace.

Something tells me this isn't the last we'll see of the visitors.

"Eden, how did you survive?"

Warden approaches from behind and wraps his arms around me.

"I'm sorry about Elvandra. We were too late," I say. "Thanks to Rachana though, I can live another day. Long enough to say goodbye for real this time."

"What? No, you can't go now. If you let Czar amputate you can stay with us. *We'll* protect you."

"No, Warden. I'm a danger to myself and to my friends. This is my fight. You've each saved my life so it's time I saved my own."

Warden lowers his head and then follows a trail of

blood to the last guard Rachana murdered. His eyes widen at the destruction of the courtyard and the pile of bodies we left behind.

"Rachana stole explosives from their armoury," I tell him. "She came back for me."

"That's one brave kid," he says, laughing. "I can't believe it. We're free."

"For now but they'll be back."

"I'm sure. So now what?" he says.

Our people begin to flow out of the cell block and into the courtyard. The once fresh white snow quickly becomes blood-spattered and brown from their filth, but the smiles on their faces are enough to know we've succeeded this time. Victory is ours and now it's up to us to ensure it stays that way.

Ginny wraps Rachana in a tight hold and joins our group. "Mika tells me there are wreckages that will offer shelter and safety from mutants until darkness finds it."

"You mean it's in the daylight?"

Mika nods and smiles. "At the moment, and likely for another few months. If we can get our people there and re-build, I think we have a good chance at surviving. We could create a new Titan."

"In three months? Is that possible?" Warden asks.

"I think you've proven yourselves worthy," I say, raising unexpected smiles from my friends.

I pick up my pack and soak in their voices, their scents and the memories of their good nature to take with me on my journey.

"Whatever you do, and wherever you decide to settle, I'll never be too far away."

"Thank you," says Czar. "For freeing us all."

"I'm sorry for trying to kill you. Twice." I laugh, and the group laugh with me. "Though you deserved it both times."

When we settle and the silence becomes too unbearable, I hand Warden the documents and insist he burn any evidence of the alien's presence here on Earth.

"Are you sure? We won't have evidence for anyone we save."

"Absolutely," I say. "If we have to begin again, so do they. Besides, you can convince them to follow you. You're good people."

Warden smiles and hands the paperwork to Czar, then takes hold of my hand.

"It is hereby decreed," he begins, "that Daemon Czar and his descendants shall rule, *Aeon Infinitum*, the survivors of the ark Titan in the event of societal destruction, natural disaster and/ or an apocalyptic event."

"Including aliens," I add, and Warden laughs.

"Yeah," he says, "including aliens."

About The Author

E. Rachael Hardcastle is multi-genre fiction author from West Yorkshire, England.

Rachael believes that through writing we face our darkest fears, explore infinite new worlds and realise our true purpose. She writes to entertain and share important morals and values with the world, but above all, she writes to be a significant part of something incredible. Her novels face our planet's struggles because she believes that together we can build a stronger future for the human race.

www.erachaelhardcastle.com.

Lightning Source UK Ltd.
Milton Keynes UK
UKHW010947190619
344666UK00001BA/6/P